OTHERWISE KNOWN AS
SHEILA THE GREAT

Books by Judy Blume

The One in the Middle Is the Green Kangaroo
Freckle Juice

The Pain and the Great One series
Soupy Saturdays
Cool Zone
Going, Going, Gone!
Friend or Fiend?

The Fudge books
Tales of a Fourth Grade Nothing
Otherwise Known as Sheila the Great
Superfudge
Fudge-a-Mania
Double Fudge

For 9+ readers
Blubber
Iggie's House
Starring Sally J. Freedman as Herself
Are You There, God? It's Me, Margaret
It's Not the End of the World
Then Again, Maybe I Won't
Deenie
Just as Long as We're Together
Here's to You, Rachel Robinson

For teens
Tiger Eyes
Forever
Letters to Judy: What Kids Wish They Could Tell You

Judy Blume

A FUDGE BOOK

OTHERWISE KNOWN AS SHEILA THE GREAT

MACMILLAN CHILDREN'S BOOKS

in association with The Bodley Head

First published in Great Britain 1979 by The Bodley Head Limited
First published 1980 in Piccolo by Pan Books
Published 2003 by Macmillan Children's Books

This edition published 2014 by Macmillan Children's Books
an imprint of Pan Macmillan
20 New Wharf Road, London N1 9RR
Associated companies throughout the world
www.panmacmillan.com

ISBN 978-1-4472-6293-0

3 5 7 9 8 6 4

A CIP catalogue record for this book is available from
the British Library.

Printed and bound by CPI Group (UK) Ltd, Croydon CR0 4YY

*In loving memory of my father
and our special game of hide-and-seek*

Contents

1

Summer in Tarrytown

I'm glad there's only one more week of school before summer vacation. Today was so hot! My clothes stuck to me and my brain felt all tired out. I didn't even finish my maths in school. So now I have to do it for homework.

I walked into the lobby of my apartment building thinking how good a big, cold drink would taste. I pushed the Up elevator button and waited. When the elevator got to the lobby Henry opened the gate and I stepped in. Just as he was about to take me upstairs Peter Hatcher and his dumb old dog came tearing down the hall.

'Wait up, Henry!' Peter called. 'Here I come.'

'Please don't wait, Henry,' I said. 'The

1

elevator's too small for that dog.'

But Henry opened the gate and waited. 'This elevator can hold ten people or the equivalent,' Henry said. 'And I figure that dog is the equivalent of a person and a half. So with me and you and Peter and that dog we've still only got four and a half people.'

Sometimes I wish Henry didn't spend so much time thinking.

'Hi, Henry,' Peter said. 'Thanks for waiting.'

'Any time, Peter,' Henry told him.

'Excuse me, please,' I said, stepping out of the elevator. I held my nose. 'I can't ride up with that dog. He stinks!'

My heart was beating so loud I was sure Henry and Peter could hear it. And I know Turtle, the dog, was laughing at me. He stuck out his tongue and licked the corner of his mouth. I'll bet he could taste me already! I walked down the hall with my head held high, saying, 'P.U.'

Henry called, 'Ten flights up is a long walk, Sheila.'

'I don't mind,' I called back.

Henry was right. Ten flights up *is* a long walk. By the time I got to my floor I was huffing and puffing so hard I had to sit down on the landing and rest. Little drips of sweat ran from my face down to my neck. Still, I think it's pretty smart of me to pretend that I hate Turtle because he smells. I always hold my nose when I see Peter coming with him. That way Peter will never know the truth!

After a few minutes I wiped my face with the back of my hand and walked down the hall to our apartment. Mrs Reese is the only person on our floor with a dog. And I don't worry too much about her. Because her dog is so small she carries him around in her arms. She calls him Baby and knits him little

sweaters to wear in the winter.

I pushed open our apartment door and went straight into the kitchen to get something to drink.

'Is that you, Sheila?' my mother called.

'Yes,' I answered.

'Did you have fun at Laurie's?'

'Yes,' I said, gulping down a whole can of apple juice.

'Is it still hot out?' Mom asked.

'Yes.'

'Did you remember to bring home a quart of milk?'

Oh oh! I knew I forgot something.

'Sheila . . . did you bring home the milk?' Mom called again.

'No . . . I forgot.'

I went into the living room then. My mother was reading a book. The record player was on and my sister Libby was twirling around in her

pink toe slippers. She is thirteen and thinks she's a great ballerina. I could hold my nose for the way Libby dances, but I'd get into big trouble if I did.

My mother said, 'You better go back down and get the milk, Sheila.'

I flopped into the big chair that tilts back and said, 'I can't, Mom. I'm dead. I just walked up the stairs.'

'Don't tell me the elevator is out of order!' Mom said.

'No.'

'Then why did you walk up ten flights of stairs?'

'I don't know,' I said. 'I just felt like it.'

'Sheila, that was a very foolish thing to do in this heat,' Mom told me. 'Now go into your room and lie down for a while before supper.'

'Do I have to?' I asked.

5

'Yes, you do. Libby will go to the store and get the milk.'

Libby did three flying leaps before she said, 'Can't you see I'm in the middle of a record?'

'The record can wait,' Mom said. 'I need the milk for supper and Daddy will be home soon.'

'But, Mother! I'm in my leotard,' Libby said.

Libby used to say Mom, like me. But since she started junior high it's Mother this and Mother that. She is very strange.

Mom told Libby, 'You can put a skirt over your leotard and nobody will notice.' Then she looked at me. 'Sheila, what are you waiting for? I said go and lie down.'

'OK . . . OK,' I said. 'I'm going.' I took off my shoes and arranged them on the floor so that the toes pointed towards my bedroom.

I line them up every day before my father comes home. It's part of a private game Daddy and I play. I am always hiding somewhere

and Daddy has to find me. His only clue is my shoes. I invented this game when I was seven and we've been playing it ever since.

Libby says when she was ten she acted a lot more grown-up than me. I think she missed out on some good fun. Anyway, Daddy would be disappointed if I stopped playing our game.

Libby and I share a bedroom. I stretched out on my bed while Libby turned the closet upside down looking for a skirt.

'You are a pain!' she said to me. 'You know that, Sheila? You are a real live *pain*!'

I didn't answer her.

'Why'd you walk up the stairs . . . huh?'

I still didn't answer.

'Did you see a dog in the elevator? I'll bet that's it. I'll bet Mrs Reese was in the elevator with Baby.'

'Wrong!' I said.

Libby finally found a skirt and pulled it

on over her leotard. 'Then I'll bet it was Peter Hatcher and Turtle.'

'Maybe it was and maybe it wasn't,' I said.

'*Chicken chicken chicken*,' Libby called as she left.

I put my hands over my ears to show I wasn't even listening.

Libby got back with the milk right before Daddy got home for supper. I jumped off my bed and crawled under it when I heard him say, 'Hello, I'm home.'

I knew Daddy found my shoes when he called, 'Ah ha! I'm coming to find a Sheila!'

It really isn't very hard for him to find me. There aren't that many places where I can hide. We only have five rooms. Still, Daddy always pretends he doesn't have any idea where I might be.

When he came into my room he started

opening my dresser drawers. He said, 'Hmmm, no Sheila in here. No Sheila in there either.'

I laughed. Daddy knows I wouldn't fit into a dresser drawer. And as soon as I laughed he lifted my bedspread and looked under the bed.

'Ah ha! I found a Sheila!'

I crawled out and kissed Daddy hello. Libby walked in then. 'I don't think you should encourage her to be such a baby,' she told Daddy.

'I am not a baby!' I shouted.

'Then why don't you stop playing baby games?' Libby asked.

'All right, Libby,' Daddy said. 'That's enough!'

'You see,' Libby said. 'You're always on *her* side!'

'I'm not on anyone's side,' Daddy said. 'Let's forget about this and go and have our supper. I've got some news for you.'

I was sure Daddy's news would be about our summer plans. We've been waiting and waiting to find out what we're going to do this summer. I wanted to take a trip to Disneyland but Mom and Daddy said, *That's out of the question.*

When we sat down at the table and started to eat Daddy said, 'We got the house!'

'Oh, Buzz,' Mom said. 'That's wonderful!'

I wish people would stop calling my father Buzz and start calling him Bertram. That's his real name. I feel so silly having a father named Buzz.

'What house?' Libby asked.

'In Tarrytown,' Daddy told her. 'It belongs to a professor at Marymount who's spending the summer in England.'

My father is a professor at Marymount College too. He teaches English. Libby says when she is old enough to go to college she is

not going to Marymount because there aren't enough boys around there. Libby thinks boys are *very* important. Libby is sick!

'It sounds nice,' Mom said. 'Anything's better than the city in July and August.'

'I hope there's something to do in Tarrytown,' Libby said. 'I really wanted to go to the beach this summer.'

I happen to know that is because Libby has a new bikini and she wants to show it off.

'You'll like Tarrytown,' Daddy told Libby. 'There's a pool down the road from our house and there's a very good day camp . . .'

Libby interrupted. 'I'm much too old for day camp, Father! You know that.'

'Not this one,' Daddy said. 'It's special. You can't even go if you're not at least ten. It's a cultural arts camp.'

'I'm no good at art, Father. You know that too,' Libby said.

'Art includes theatre, music *and* dancing,' Daddy told her.

'Dancing?' Libby asked.

Then Mom and Daddy got these big smiles on their faces. I'm sure they knew all along that Libby would be very happy once she found out she could spend the summer on her dumb old toes!

'Oh, Father . . . oh, Mother!' Libby cried.

'I wanted to go to Disneyland,' I said.

'We told you that was out of the question,' Mom said.

'I know. But I still wanted to go.'

'In Tarrytown you can have your own bedroom,' Daddy said.

'I can?'

'Yes. There are four bedrooms in Professor Egran's house.'

I thought that over. *My own bedroom*. That sounded pretty good.

'And you can learn to swim,' Mom said.

'I don't want to learn to swim,' I told her.

'We'll see,' she said. 'We don't have to decide now.'

'Can my bedroom be far away from Libby's?'

'We'll see about that too,' Mom said. 'Now finish your string beans.'

The next day I told Peter Hatcher, 'I'm going away for the whole summer. I'm going to have my own bedroom.'

'Goody for you!' he said.

'So you don't have to wash your dog. Because I won't be around to tell you how bad he smells!'

'My dog said to tell you he thinks you smell too,' Peter said. Then he went off with Jimmy Fargo and they both laughed and laughed. They think they're so funny! I don't know why I used to waste my time playing 'cooties' with them. Maybe next year I'll get lucky. Maybe

13

Peter Hatcher and Jimmy Fargo won't be in my fifth-grade class.

I met Mrs Reese in the hall. 'I'm going away for the whole summer,' I said. 'I'm going to have my own bedroom, with flowered wallpaper and frilly curtains and little lamps shaped like candles.'

And she said, 'Aren't you lucky! Baby would like to go away too, but he doesn't have any place to go.'

I told Henry I'd be away for two whole months. 'I'm going to sleep in my own bedroom, in my own canopy bed!'

Henry said, 'I'll really miss you, Sheila. Who's going to remind me how many people the elevator can hold?'

Henry and I laughed together. 'And did I tell you about the rug on my bedroom floor?' I asked.

'No,' Henry said. 'You didn't mention that.'

'Well, it's very soft and fluffy and it's all yellow except for a big red rose right in the centre. It feels so good on your feet you never have to wear slippers. Not all summer long.'

'That sounds mighty nice, Sheila.'

I thought so too. The more I talked about it the better it sounded. Spending the summer in the country. Spending the summer in Tarrytown. Spending the summer in a house. Spending the summer in my own beautiful bedroom!

It started to sound almost as good as going to Disneyland. I didn't even mind the packing and the ride to Tarrytown. I couldn't wait to see the house. I couldn't wait to see my bedroom.

And then I found out about Jennifer.

2
Jennifer!

Jennifer is small with brown and white spots and long ears. When Libby saw her she cried, 'Oh, what an adorable dog!'

'She comes with the house,' Daddy said. 'She belongs to Professor Egran and she's ours for the summer.'

'I'm going back to the car,' I said.

Daddy held my arm. 'She can't hurt you.'

'Oh sure,' I said, pulling away from him. 'But I'll just wait in the car until you decide what to do with her. Because *I'm* not staying here if *she* does!' I ran down to the road, jumped into our car, and started to shake. How could they do this to me? Their own child. Their own younger daughter. Didn't they understand? Didn't they care?

Daddy and Mom hurried to the car. Mom stuck her head in the open window. 'Sheila,' she said, 'Jennifer is very small. She's more afraid of you than you are of her.'

'Did she tell you that?' I asked.

Daddy said, 'She's got a doghouse and a fenced-in area. She's chained up. You don't have to go near her.'

'Suppose she gets away?' I asked. 'Suppose her chain breaks?'

'That won't happen,' Daddy said. 'But even if it did, someone would catch her.'

'You're just saying that!' I told Daddy. 'But you don't mean it.'

'Have we ever lied to you?' Mom asked.

'Well . . . no.'

'Then trust us,' Daddy said.

I looked out of the car window. Libby was cuddling Jennifer. 'You promise she'll never come into the house?'

'I promise,' Daddy said. 'She's got everything she needs outside.'

'And you won't make me go near her?'

'Of course not,' Mom said. 'You can even pretend she's not there if you want.'

'And you won't make fun of me?'

'Do we ever make fun of you?' Daddy asked.

'Libby does,' I said.

'We'll see that she doesn't,' Mom promised.

'Now, don't you want to come into the house and see your very own bedroom?' Daddy asked.

'Well . . . I guess so,' I said, getting out of the car.

We walked up the front lawn to the house. Libby was still holding Jennifer. When Jennifer saw me coming she jumped off Libby's lap. She barked and barked.

'You see!' I cried, turning around, ready to run back to the car. 'She hates me already!'

'Don't be silly,' Daddy said. He took my hand.

'I'm not being silly. Why else would she bark like that?'

'Because she doesn't know you,' Mom said, putting an arm around me.

'And she's never going to, either. I'll tell you that!'

We went into the house. The downstairs looked pretty nice, but I wanted to see my bedroom. So Daddy and I went upstairs while Libby and Mom poked around in the kitchen.

Daddy turned right at the top of the stairs and walked down the hall. 'Two of the bedrooms are this way and the other two are that way,' Daddy said, pointing. 'Since you wanted to be far away from Libby I thought you might like this one.' Daddy pushed open a door and smiled.

I went in. The first thing I saw was the dresser.

It was piled with models of planes, boats and cars. And the walls were full of team pennants. There wasn't even a bedspread on the bed. Just an ugly old grey blanket with CAMP KENABEC printed across it. I opened the closet door. The shelves were loaded with sports equipment. And where was my soft, fluffy, yellow rug with the big rose in the middle? No place. The floor was bare!

Daddy said, 'Well . . .'

'I hate it!' I shouted, running out of the room, past Daddy, and down the hall. I looked into the other bedrooms. But they were all the same.

'They're all boys' rooms!' I cried.

Daddy followed me and said, 'Well, of course they are. Professor Egran has three sons.'

When I heard that I got so mad I kicked a closet door and made a mark on it. Mom came upstairs then and said that wasn't a very nice

thing to do in somebody else's house. Maybe it wasn't, but I didn't care.

Libby wasn't disappointed when she saw her bedroom. She doesn't mind having a boy's room. She loves it! She says it makes her feel very close to Professor Egran's fifteen-year-old son. Daddy says my room belongs to his twelve-year-old son. But if I hate it that much I can have the room which belongs to his three-year-old son, even though it's much smaller. I told him, 'No thank you. I'd rather sleep in a twelve-year-old's room than one that belongs to a baby.'

Mom said if we hurried and unpacked we could go for a ride around Tarrytown. So I went to my room and put my clothes away. When I opened the desk drawers I found six tubes of Testor's glue, twenty-seven bottles of model paint and a note. It said:

WARNING TO WHOEVER USES THIS
ROOM. I HATE GIRLS! SO IF YOU ARE
ONE LOOK OUT!

AND IF YOU TOUCH ANY OF MY
MODELS I WILL GET YOU SOMEDAY!!!

B. E.

'Ha ha ha,' I said, ripping the note into tiny pieces.

After supper Daddy drove us around Tarrytown. It is a very hilly place. When you get up high you can look down and see the Hudson River. Of course you can also see it right in New York City. When I was younger I used to climb to the top of the jungle gym and look out at it. There is something about the Hudson River that makes you feel good, even if it is polluted.

When we came home I got ready for bed. Before I climbed in I looked out of my window.

And what was right underneath my room? *Jennifer.* That dumb old dog! She looked up at me and barked. I barked right back at her. I knew we should have gone to Disneyland.

3
Noises in the Night

I got into bed. My room was very dark. I'm not used to sleeping all by myself in the dark. I closed my eyes but nothing happened. So I got out of bed and turned on the light. That was a little better. Soon the house was quiet. I knew everyone else was sound asleep. I tossed around for a while. Then I tried lying on my back. I looked up at the ceiling. I tried to think of something funny. Something that would give me a good dream.

That's when I saw the spider. He was running across my ceiling. I hate spiders! One time Peter Hatcher put a fake spider in my desk at school. When I took out my English book, there it was. But I knew it was a phony right away. So I held

it by one leg and took it up to Mrs Haver. 'Just look what Peter Hatcher put inside my desk,' I said, shaking the spider.

Mrs Haver screamed so loud she scared the whole class. And Peter Hatcher had to stay after school for three days!

I looked at my ceiling again. The spider was still there and *this* one was no phony. 'Go away, spider!' I whispered. 'Please go away and don't come back.' But the spider didn't move. He was right over my head. Suppose he falls on me, I thought. Suppose he's the poisonous kind and when he falls he bites me. Maybe I should put my head under the covers. Then if he falls on me it won't matter. No, that's no good either. He could crawl inside the covers and get me anyway. I could just picture Peter Hatcher telling the kids at school, *Did you hear about Sheila Tubman? She got bitten by a poisonous spider on her first night in Tarrytown. In twenty seconds she was dead!*

I jumped out of bed and ran down the hall to my parents' room. Daddy was snoring. I touched him on the shoulder. He sat right up in the bed. 'What? What is it?' he asked.

'It's just me, Daddy,' I told him.

'Sheila . . . what do you want? It's the middle of the night.'

'I can't sleep, Daddy. There's a spider on my ceiling.'

Mom rolled over. She made a noise like *ummm*.

'Shush,' Daddy said. 'Go back to bed. I'll get it in the morning.'

'But, Daddy, he could fall on me. Maybe he's poisonous.'

'Oh . . . all right,' Daddy said, kicking off the covers.

We walked down the hall together. 'How did you notice a spider on your ceiling in the

middle of the night?' Daddy asked.

'I have my light on.'

Daddy didn't ask why.

When we got to my room he said, 'OK, where's your spider?'

At first I didn't see him. But then he started running across my ceiling. 'There he is!' I pointed. 'You see?'

Daddy picked up one of my shoes.

'Hurry,' I said.

Daddy stood on my bed, but when he smacked my shoe against the ceiling the spider ran the other way.

I tried to help. I gave him directions. 'That's it,' I called. 'Now just a little to the left. No, no, now to the right. Hit him, Daddy! Hit him now!'

But Daddy missed him every time. He was running up and down my bed, but the spider ran faster.

Just as Daddy said, 'I give up,' he got him.

27

Squish . . . that was the end of my spider. There was a big black mark on the ceiling. But I felt a whole lot better.

'Now, would you please go back to sleep!' Daddy said.

'I'll try.'

'And if you find anything else unusual . . . tell me about it in the morning.'

'OK,' I said, snuggling under the covers.

I think I fell asleep then. But a few hours later I woke up. I heard this really scary noise. It sounded like *whooo whooo whooo*. I didn't know what to do. I buried my head under the pillow, but that didn't help. I could still hear it. I thought about what it might be – a ghost, or a vampire, or even an ordinary monster.

I got up and ran back down the hall. Daddy was snoring much louder now. This time I walked around to Mom's side of the bed and shook her a little. She jumped up.

'Oh, Sheila!' she said, when she saw who it was. 'You scared me!'

'I'm sorry,' I whispered.

'What is it?'

'It's a noise in my room,' I said.

'Go back to sleep,' Mom told me. 'It's nothing.'

'How do you know?' I asked. 'You haven't heard it. It sounds like a ghost.'

'There aren't any ghosts!'

'Please, Mom, please come and see.'

'Oh . . . all right.' She put on her robe and we went down the hall to my room. 'Well,' Mom said, 'where's your noise?'

'Just wait,' I told her.

She sat down on my bed and yawned. Soon it started again. *Whooo . . . whooo . . .*

'You see?' I said, throwing my arms around Mom. I could tell from her face that she didn't like the noise either. 'You want me to go wake Daddy?' I asked.

'No, not yet,' Mom said. 'First I'll have a look around myself. Hand me that baseball bat in the corner.'

'For what?' I asked.

'Just in case,' Mom said.

I gave Mom the bat. She held it like she was ready to use it.We waited until we heard the noise again. *Whooo . . . whooo . . . whooo . . .*

'That's coming from outside,' Mom said.

'So it's an outside ghost,' I told her.

She went to the window. She stood there for a minute before she started to laugh.

'What's funny?' I asked.

'Oh, Sheila . . . just look!'

I hid behind her and peeked out of the window. There was a beautiful silver moon. And there was also Jennifer, with her head held high. *She* was making those noises.

'What is she doing?' I asked. 'Is she crazy?'

'She's baying at the moon,' Mom said.

'What's baying?'

'It's like singing.'

'You mean she is going to stand there and make that ghost noise all summer?'

'I think so,' Mom said.

'I told you to get rid of her, didn't I?' I said. 'Who needs her? Who needs her making scary noises at me?'

'Come on, Sheila,' Mom said, putting the baseball bat back in the corner. 'Get into bed.'

She tucked me in. I felt very tired.

'Now go to sleep.'

'I'll try,' I said.

When Mom left I heard the noise again. *Whooo whooo whooo.*

'Oh shut up, you dumb old dog!' I called.

And she did.

4

Junior Yo-Yo Champion

The next day I met Mouse Ellis. She is also ten and going into fifth grade. I was sitting on the front steps wondering what to do until it was time to go and register for day camp. Then I saw this girl walking up the road. I watched until she got to the front of my house. She looked at me and waved. I waved back.

She came up our driveway and over to where I was sitting. She held up a purple yo-yo. 'I'm Mouse Ellis, Junior Champion of Tarrytown,' she said. 'I can do eleven different tricks without stopping. How many can you do?'

'I never stopped to count,' I told her.

She opened her eyes very wide and offered me her yo-yo. 'Go ahead and show me,' she said.

'I don't feel like it.'

I'll bet you can't do Shotgun six times in a row.'

'I'll bet I can,' I told her.

'OK, let's see you do it then.'

'After you,' I said.

'OK.' Mouse wound up her yo-yo, held it close to her hip, and next thing I knew, out it flew, right at me, six times in a row.

'Very good,' I said.

She handed me her yo-yo. I examined it all over.

'It's a Duncan Imperial,' she told me. 'The very best yo-yo made.'

'It's not bad,' I said.

'I'm ready any time you are,' Mouse said.

I stood up, held the yo-yo to my hip, threw it out, and whacked myself in the head on my first try.

'Hey, are you OK?' Mouse asked.

33

'Oh sure,' I told her. 'But I guess I'll have to tell you the truth now. I didn't want to hurt your feelings before. But where I come from, yo-yos are for babies. I haven't done Shotgun for about eight years now. That's why I missed.'

Mouse looked at me for a while and I gave her one of my best stares right back. Then she sat down next to me and said, 'You'll never know how glad I am that you moved in for the summer. I'm so sick of those Egran boys!'

I couldn't help smiling. She wouldn't have stayed if she didn't believe I really was a yo-yoer when I was a little kid. 'I'm sleeping in one of the Egran boys' bedrooms,' I said. 'And guess what I found in the desk?'

'What?' Mouse asked.

'Six tubes of Testor's glue and twenty-seven jars of model paint!'

Mouse laughed. 'You must have Bobby's room. He's a model maniac.'

34

'He left a note for me,' I said. 'He signed it B.E.'

'That's Bobby!'

'He wrote that if I touch any of his models he'll get me some day.'

'Ha ha!' Mouse said. 'He's all talk.'

'That's what I figured. Anyway, who'd want to fool around with his dumb old models?'

'Not me,' Mouse said. 'I've got better things to do.'

'Me too. Say, is your real name Mouse?'

'No, it's Merle, but everybody calls me Mouse.'

'You better watch out,' I said. 'My father's name is really Bertram and everybody *still* calls him Buzz.'

'Well, I don't care if people call me Mouse forever. I like it a whole lot better than Merle. And if you ask me, Buzz is a much better name than Bertram. Bertram sounds awful. Nothing

against your father, of course.'

'I didn't mean that I don't like your nickname,' I said. 'As long as you *like* to be called Mouse. Personally I think it's a very nice name. It's much better than Sheila.'

'If you don't like Sheila you should call yourself something else,' Mouse said.

'Like what?' I asked.

'Oh . . . maybe Sugar or Sunny or something like that.'

'I don't like Sugar,' I said. 'But Sunny sounds pretty good. Sunny Tubman . . . yeah, I kind of like that.'

'OK, then that's what I'll call you from now on,' Mouse said.

I told Mouse about Libby then, and how she says *Mother* and *Father* and pretends to be very grown-up. And Mouse told me about her little sister Betsy, who still wets the bed every night. We found out we are both going to the same

day camp and the same pool.

In a little while Mouse stood up and started to yo-yo again, and I could see why she is Junior Champion of Tarrytown. While she was showing me her tricks I noticed that her legs were a mess of scabs. I hoped they weren't catching.

She must have seen me looking because she said, 'They're leftover mosquito bites. I scratch them until they bleed and then I get scabs. Aren't they ugly?'

I didn't tell her the truth. I said, 'They're not so bad.'

When Mouse was done with her yo-yo tricks she said, 'Let's take Jennifer for a walk.'

'Jennifer the dog, you mean?'

'Yes. The Egrans always let me walk her. I love dogs.'

I never make friends with dog-lovers. 'Do you have one at your house?' I asked, thinking

I might as well find out the truth right away. There was no point in getting to like her if it was all for nothing.

'No,' Mouse said. 'Betsy is allergic to them. She gets hives from dogs.'

What a great idea. Why didn't I ever think of saying that? 'Me too,' I told Mouse. 'I get awful hives from them. You wouldn't believe how big my hives are. They'd make your scabs look practically invisible, they're so huge!'

'Oh, rats!' Mouse said. 'I was hoping you and me could take care of Jennifer all summer.'

'I'm really sorry,' I said.

'Oh, that's OK. I guess I'd rather have a girlfriend than a dog.'

I was very happy to hear that.

We walked down the road to her house then. Mouse yo-yoed all the way. She lives at the bottom of the hill, right around the corner from

the swimming pool. Her little sister was out front dragging a candy box by a string.

'That's Betsy,' Mouse said. 'She's four.'

'Why does she have a string around that box?'

'She's walking her dog.'

'That box is her dog?' I asked.

'Yes. I told you how she gets hives from real ones. So that box is her pretend dog. She calls it Ootch.'

Betsy dragged Ootch over to us. 'Who are you?' she asked me.

'I'm Sunny Tubman,' I told her, trying out my new name.

'Oh. You don't look like a boy,' Betsy said.

'She's not a boy!' Mouse told her.

'Then how come her name is Sonny?'

'It's not that kind of Sonny,' Mouse explained. 'It's Sunny, like the sun in the sky.'

'Ohhh,' Betsy said. 'Sunny like a sunny day?'

'That's it,' Mouse said.

'My real name is Sheila,' I said to Betsy. 'Maybe you should call me that.' I didn't think about Sunny sounding like Sonny. Maybe it wasn't such a good name after all.

Betsy said, 'This is my dog, Ootch. Want to pet him?'

'Oh sure.' I reached over and tapped the candy box. 'Nice doggie,' I said. 'Nice Ootch.'

Betsy picked up her box and held it to her ear. Then she put it back down and said, 'Ootch says he likes you, Sunny Sheila. He can always tell a person who really and truly loves dogs.'

I didn't say anything. I just smiled.

Mrs Ellis invited me to stay for lunch. I phoned home and Mom said I could. Me and Mouse ate peanut butter sandwiches with the crust cut off and Betsy had four slices of plain salami – no bread or anything. She kept Ootch on the table next to her and every few minutes

she made believe she was feeding some of her salami to that box.

'Ootch loves salami,' she told me. 'It's his favourite lunch.'

That afternoon our mothers took us to the Cultural Arts Centre to register for day camp. It is really a private school, but it doesn't look anything like one. It looks like an old house surrounded by lots and lots of big trees. I have never seen a school like that. Mouse told me that she doesn't go there. She goes to regular junior school. But Bobby Egran has been going there for years. That's because Bobby refused to do any of his work in junior school. All he wanted to do was build models. And since the teachers wouldn't let him he used to get mad and make a lot of noise. So he was spending most of his time sitting on the bench outside the principal's office. At this school he is allowed to

build all kinds of things. Mouse says her mother told her Bobby is some kind of genius but she doesn't believe it.

Mouse and I explored our day camp together. This is her first year too because she is just ten, which means me and Mouse will be two of the youngest kids there. This makes Libby feel like a double big shot! I told Mouse that Libby thinks she is a great ballerina but when she dances she really looks like an elephant. Well, not exactly an elephant, but only because she is too skinny to be one.

There are a lot of interesting activities at this day camp. But the one that looks best to me is pottery. You get to use a lot of mushy clay and you try to shape it into some kind of bowl on a pottery wheel. Me and Mouse signed up for that, first thing. The pottery counsellor's name is Denise. She was barefoot. I like to go barefoot too, but I'm afraid I might step on a bee and get

stung. That happened to Peter Hatcher's little brother once. I think getting stung on the bottom of your foot would be worse than getting stung some place ordinary, like your arm. I wonder if Denise has ever stepped on a bee.

When we got home Mouse asked me to go swimming with her. She said, 'What's your best stroke? Mine's the crawl.'

'I'm the same at every stroke,' I said.

'Then maybe you'll join the swimming team. We have races every Sunday.'

She didn't understand what I meant, I guess. So I said, 'No, I really don't like swimming teams. They take all the fun out of it.'

'Well, grab your suit and let's go over anyway. It's steaming out.'

'I can't go in today,' I said. I wasn't about to tell her I can't swim.

'Why can't you go in?' she asked.

'I'm just getting over a cold.'

'Oh, rats! You don't sound sick. Ask your mother.'

'I can't,' I said. 'I promised I wouldn't go in today.'

'Can't you even dunk your feet?' Mouse asked.

That didn't sound bad. And it was hot out. 'OK,' I said. 'I guess dunking my feet can't hurt me. I'll go in and get my suit.'

But just then my mother came out and said, 'Sheila, we have to go over to the pool now. I want to sign you up for some lessons. It's time you learned how to swim!'

Mouse opened her mouth, but nothing came out.

5

Anybody Can Learn to Swim

'How could you do that to me?' I asked my mother when we were alone.

'I'm sorry,' Mom said. 'I didn't know she thought you could swim.'

'You just spoiled my whole summer!'

'Oh really, Sheila! Let's not make a big thing out of it.'

'Just when she wanted to be my friend – my first real-live girlfriend. You had to go and ruin everything! Well, I'm *never* going to learn how to swim. So there!'

'You have to, like it or not!' Mom said. 'Otherwise it isn't safe to go near the water.'

'I'll never go near the water. Then you won't have to worry.'

45

'Daddy and I have discussed it and we both agree that you must learn to swim. Even if it takes all summer. And that's that!'

'You can't make me!' I cried.

'Sheila, you are being unreasonable. Daddy and I try very hard to be understanding. We don't force you to go near Jennifer. We know how you feel about spiders, and when you hear noises in the middle of the night we try to find out what's causing them. *But we are going to insist that you learn how to swim!*'

'I'll sink,' I said. 'They'll find me on the bottom of the pool and that will be the end of me.'

'I don't think that will happen,' Mom said. 'Now get into the car.'

Mom tooted the horn and Libby came running out of the house. She was wearing her bikini. She looked like a skeleton.

'Can we take Jennifer with us?' Libby asked.

'No,' I said.

'I'm not asking *you*. Can we, Mom? I'll bet she's dying for a little ride in the car.'

'You promised!' I reminded my mother.

'Better leave her at home, Libby,' Mom said.

'Some people spoil all the fun!' Libby snapped.

'There are people who get hives from dogs,' I told Libby. 'Did you ever think of that?'

'But *you* don't!'

'I think I do.'

'You're a liar,' Libby yelled. 'Isn't she a liar, Mom?'

'What do you mean you think you get hives from dogs?' Mom asked me.

'I do. I get them inside where you can't see them. But I know they're there. I'm positive I'm allergic to dogs.'

'Oh, Sheila!' Mom said.

Jennifer stood up and barked then. I'm sure

she was laughing at me. I hate that dumb old dog!

Libby sulked all the way to the pool because Mom told her Jennifer had to stay at home. She said this had nothing to do with me. It was just that there was probably a rule about bringing animals to the pool. I don't think Libby believed Mom, but she seemed to forget about it when we got there.

The swimming pool is round at the deep end and curved at the other. My mother says it is kidney-shaped. I wonder if my kidneys are shaped like that. When I get home I will look it up in my encyclopedia and find out. There are two diving boards. One is up high and the other is medium.

Each family has a tiny dressing room with their name on the door. Ours says Egran. I asked, 'Couldn't we put up a little sign that says Tubman . . . just for the summer?' I felt silly

using the Egrans' dressing room. I kept thinking about those three boys. So my mother let me Scotch tape TUBMAN over EGRAN so at least people will know who we are.

Libby doesn't care about going to the beach any more. Because the pool is full of boys. Besides the lifeguards and the pool boys who work there, plenty of other boys come just to swim. My sister, in her new bikini, thinks she is just the greatest!

But after she saw my swimming teacher she asked my mother to sign her up for lessons too. My teacher, Marty, is what Libby calls *terrific*. I do not care one way or the other what my swimming teacher looks like. Because I don't ever want to swim. I know I won't be able to. I know I will sink to the bottom and everyone will laugh and Marty will have to save me.

I told him this right off, when my mother

signed me up for fifteen private lessons.

'I'll never be able to swim,' I said.

'Sure you will,' Marty told me.

'No, I mean it! I won't!'

'Anybody can learn to swim,' Marty said.

'Well, I'm never going to put my face in the water. I'll tell you that!'

'Sure you will. It's easy. There's nothing to be afraid of.'

'Afraid! Me? Is that what you think?'

Marty just smiled.

'I'm not afraid of anything!' I told him. 'Nothing! I just think it's dumb of my mother to waste her money on swimming lessons. Because if I felt like it I could jump right in and swim as good as anybody!'

'That's great,' Marty said. 'Tomorrow you can show me how you do that.'

I didn't answer him.

*

That night Libby begged my parents for swimming lessons.

'You swim very well now,' Mom told her.

'But think of all Marty could teach me,' Libby said.

'You don't need him to teach you anything,' Daddy told her. 'Now that's that!'

'Sheila gets all the good things!' Libby cried. 'It's not fair.'

'You can have my lessons,' I said. 'All fifteen of them.'

But Daddy and Mom said, 'Oh no!' together.

The next afternoon I told Mom that I had an awful stomach ache and I couldn't possibly go to the pool. She gave me a spoon of pink peppermint stuff and told me I'd be fine in a few minutes.

When we got to the pool I told her I had a sore throat and that people with sore throats

51

shouldn't go swimming. Mom said it was probably just an allergy to the trees. Since when am I allergic to trees?

I told her that I forgot my bathing cap so I wouldn't be able to put my head in the water. But she pulled out a new cap and said she brought one along just in case. And then she delivered me to Marty.

He was waiting at the shallow end of the pool.

'I don't feel very well,' I told him.

'You're just nervous,' he said.

'Me, nervous? That's very funny. I never get nervous!'

'Good, I'm glad to hear that. It's much easier to work with a relaxed person than a nervous one.'

'Do nervous people sink in the water?' I asked.

'Oh . . . sometimes,' Marty said. 'But I

haven't lost more than three or four.'

I stepped away from him.

'Hey, that's a joke, Sheila!'

'I know,' I said. 'Don't you think I know a joke when I hear one?'

'Come and sit down at the edge of the pool,' Marty said, lowering himself into the water. 'I'll get wet first.'

I wished there weren't so many people around. If I had to take lessons why couldn't I take them in the middle of the night when nobody could see me?

'Now the first thing I'm going to show you is how to blow bubbles. Watch this.' Marty put his face into the water and big bubbles came up. Soon he raised his head and said, 'You see . . . you just blow bubbles. It's a cinch!'

'I told you,' I said. 'I'm not putting my face into the water.'

'I can't teach you to swim if you don't.'

'Well then, I guess you won't be able to teach me.' I stood up and started to walk away.

'Wait a minute, Sheila!' Marty reached out and grabbed my ankle. 'Get wet first . . . before you make up your mind.'

'My mind is made up,' I said.

'Well, get wet anyway. I might get fired if you don't at least get wet.'

I didn't want Marty to lose his job because of me so I walked down the three steps and stood in water up to my waist. 'It's too cold for me,' I said. 'I'll get pneumonia or something. I'm getting out!'

'Sheila! This pool must be eighty degrees today. You're not going to catch anything!'

Marty scooped me up and started walking around the pool with me.

I said, 'Put me down . . . you put me down right now or I'll scream!'

'If you do everyone will hear and look over

to see what's going on. Is that what you want?'

I think he's a mind reader. I hate him! 'What are you going to do with me?' I asked.

'Nothing. I just want you to get used to the water. And to see that I'm not going to let anything happen to you.'

'If I drown you're going to be in big trouble.'

'You're not going to drown. I already told you that. And once you learn how to swim you'll be able to save yourself so there won't be anything for you to worry about.'

'Who says I'm worried? I never worry!' I said.

'That's swell,' Marty told me.

'Did you mean it when you said if I learn to swim I'll be able to save myself?'

'Yes,' Marty said.

'Well . . . as long as I'm here I guess I might as well. So go ahead, teach me! But remember, I won't put my face in the water.'

Marty sighed. 'All right . . . I'll teach you

with your face out of the water.'

'But you said you couldn't teach me that way!'

'Well, I just remembered I can. I'll teach you to swim like a dog.'

'I don't want to swim like a dog!' I said. 'I don't even like dogs!'

'Maybe you'll like them when you learn how to swim like one,' Marty said, smiling.

He gave me a kickboard. He taught me how to hang on with my hands and kick with my legs. At first I wasn't even a good kicker. I only used one leg. I kept the other one on the bottom of the pool because I felt safer that way. I was hoping I could fool Marty into thinking I was using both of them. But it didn't work. He said, 'That's not bad, Sheila. But this time let's use both feet, OK?'

So, for the first time in my life, I took both feet off the bottom of the pool and I kicked. And

I didn't sink. But I knew that was because I was hanging on to the kickboard. If I didn't have that I'd be on the bottom in a second.

My lesson lasted half an hour and all I had to do was practise kicking. When it was over I told Marty it wasn't as bad as I thought it would be. He said he'd see me tomorrow, same time.

I ran over to my mother and she said she was proud of me, even though I didn't put my face in. I told her Marty said I didn't have to. And that I'd never have to because he was going to teach me to swim like a dog and dogs are very good swimmers . . . everyone knows that! My mother looked at me funny and said, 'Well, you and Jennifer have something in common after all, don't you?'

But I didn't answer. Because I heard someone calling, 'Sunny Sheila Tubman . . . Sunny Sheila Tubman . . . watch this!'

I looked up at the high diving board and saw

Betsy Ellis. And if Betsy was at the pool Mouse probably was too. Did she see me in the water with Marty? I hope not. But I guess now she won't want to be my friend anyway. So what's the difference if she did see me!

Betsy called me one more time, then she did a perfect dive into the water. I couldn't believe it. 'Did you see that?' I asked my mother. 'She's only four years old!'

'Beautiful, wasn't it?' Mom said. 'I hear she's a champion swimmer.'

'I don't see her anywhere,' I said, searching the pool. 'Do you suppose she's all right? Shouldn't she be up by now?'

'There she is,' Mom said, pointing. 'She swam right across underwater.'

I wondered if maybe Marty could teach me to swim like that. I could just see myself as a swimming champion. I would learn to do the most beautiful dives anyone ever saw. I would

be able to swim back and forth in the pool at least twenty times without running out of breath. Mouse would beg me to be her friend. People from all over would come to watch me on Sundays. And Marty would tell them, *She's remarkable . . . she couldn't swim at all when she came here*. And of course I would be able to do everything without ever getting my face wet. I'll bet there isn't a dog anywhere who can dive without wetting his face.

6

A Person Should Just Admit It

That night after supper, the doorbell rang. 'I'll get it,' I hollered, running to see who it was.

It was Mouse. 'Hi,' she said. 'Come on out.'

I opened the screen door and stepped outside on to the front porch.

'How was your swimming lesson?' she asked.

'It was fine,' I said. 'I used to do a lot of swimming when I was a little kid, but . . .'

Mouse didn't let me finish. 'But where you come from nobody ever goes swimming, right?'

'Kind of,' I said.

'If a person doesn't know how to do something a person should just admit it, don't you think?' Mouse said.

'Oh sure,' I told her. 'If there was something

I couldn't do I'd be the first to admit it.'

'Me too,' Mouse said. 'Like for instance, I can't turn cartwheels. I've tried and tried but I just can't get my legs up straight. Now, what can't you do?'

'Oh, I can't turn cartwheels either. At least I don't think I can. I've never even tried.'

'Try now,' Mouse said.

'Now? What for?'

'Just to see if you can or can't.'

'I can't. I'm sure I can't.'

'OK . . . there's another thing I can't do,' Mouse said. 'I can't do a backward flip into the pool.'

'Neither can I,' I told her.

'Because you can't swim . . . right?'

'Well, I don't swim much and I don't dive at all.'

'You mean you *can't*.'

'That's right,' I said. 'I can't dive at all.'

Mouse smiled. 'I brought you something.'

'You did?'

'Yes.' She reached into her pocket and held up a green yo-yo. She handed it to me. 'It's a genuine Duncan Imperial. The very best there is.'

'Thanks.' I turned it over and read what it said. 'I haven't had a yo-yo in ages.'

'Since you were about two, right?'

'That's right.'

'Tell you what,' Mouse said, 'since you don't remember much about working it, how would it be if I taught you to do tricks?'

'Well . . . I really don't need lessons because I'll probably remember how to do all my tricks as soon as I practise a little. But if you want to show me your way I wouldn't mind.'

'Good,' Mouse said. 'We'll start tomorrow. I've got to go home now. My mother doesn't like me walking around in the dark.' Mouse turned

and started down the front path.

I was already planning how I'd be able to tell the kids in the city that my own private yo-yo teacher was none other than the Junior Champion of Tarrytown herself!

The next day I asked Marty if he could teach me to dive like Betsy Ellis, but without getting my face wet.

He said, 'Impossible!'

And the more I thought about it the more I knew he was right. So I said we'd have to forget about diving. Marty asked me how I planned to get into the pool when I learned to swim and I told him, 'Down the ladder. Same as getting out.'

I spent three more days just practising how to kick. Then Marty decided it was time to learn what to do with my arms. He held me in the water and told me to move them back and forth. I was so scared I held on to Marty with

one arm and only moved the other. He said that was OK. That he had plenty of time. Two months, if necessary. Because my mother told him not to rush me. She didn't want me to get more afraid than I already was. And she said she would pay for lessons all summer if she had to. Because she had a feeling that fifteen lessons weren't going to be enough. But I'd better know how to swim by then or she'd want her money back. And Marty had promised her I would. He really needs the money for college, he told me, like I shouldn't let him down.

So I said, 'OK . . .' and I tried letting go of him. He kept his hand under me so I wouldn't get scared and stop trying. But whenever I used my arms I forgot about my legs. And when I remembered and started to kick I forgot about using my arms.

I think Marty almost gave up on me today.

After my lesson I joined Mouse and some of

the other kids. The thing I hate most is when one kid dunks another. The only way to avoid that is to stay out of the water, which is what I do. Mouse says everyone knows that I am a beginner and no one would dunk me, but I am not so sure!

Libby has a crush on a lifeguard named Freddie. He has very hairy legs. Libby says he is just the most terrific boy she has ever met. But Libby says that about *every* boy she meets. She hangs around his lifeguard chair all afternoon and when he is off duty she runs to get him a soda. My mother says he is much too old for her and she should find some friends her own age. Then Libby cries, 'But, Mother, he's only seventeen and I am practically fourteen and that's just perfect!' My mother doesn't think so. And she says if Libby keeps pestering him he could lose his job.

The Sunday after Mom said that Freddie

brought a friend to the pool. She sat next to his lifeguard chair all afternoon. She is much older than Libby. I would say she is at least sixteen. And she doesn't look like a skeleton in her bikini either.

Now Libby stays away from Freddie. She says she never really liked him anyway. And who wants a boyfriend with all that hair on his legs? 'Ha ha,' I said. Libby gave me a kick.

7
The Headless Horseman

We go to day camp every weekday, from 9.00 until 3.00. Then we go to the pool from 3.30 to 5.30. We are always so busy going somewhere that I can't believe we have been in Tarrytown for two whole weeks.

One night, before Daddy got home, I arranged my shoes in the front hall with the toes pointing towards the den. Then I hid behind the curtain and waited. But between the den and the front hall was the living room and dining room. I heard Daddy come into the house and call, 'Hello . . . I'm home.' I hoped when he saw my shoes he would come and find me right away, because there weren't any lights on in the den and the sky was getting darker

every second. It was beginning to thunder. I don't like thunderstorms. Daddy has told me a million times that the lightning isn't going to get me and I want to believe him, but I can't.

I never should have hidden so far away. I should have gone into the closet in the front hall. Then I'd have been near the kitchen, where Libby and Mom were. I wondered what was taking Daddy so long. And what were those funny noises? I wished somebody would turn on the lights.

I wasn't having fun at all! Maybe Daddy had forgotten about me. Maybe he wasn't even looking. I decided then and there that I would have to tell him I don't want to play this game any more. Not in this house! I hoped he wouldn't think it was because I'm chicken. That's what Libby would say. She'd make her cackling noise and laugh at me.

When I couldn't stand it behind the curtain

for another second I crawled out and made my way back into the living room on all fours. Finally Mom shouted, 'Sheila, come out right now or dinner will be ruined!' I was really happy when she said that. I ran into the kitchen and told Daddy if it is going to take him that long to find me every night we'll never get to eat. So he agreed that we will stop our game for the summer. Now Libby will never know the truth, so she won't have to call me chicken.

Every night after dinner Daddy unchains Jennifer and lets her run around loose. He says she needs the exercise. She tears around the yard yelping. I watch from my bedroom window. Daddy and Libby and Jennifer have a lot of fun playing games. Libby throws a ball and Jennifer catches it in her mouth. And Daddy has taught her to roll over and play dead. Both Mom and Daddy say I am silly to hide upstairs and miss all the fun. Well, maybe I am, but I

just can't help it. I wonder why I had to be born like me instead of like Libby, who isn't afraid of anything. Sometimes it doesn't seem fair.

At least I am getting used to sleeping in a room by myself. I'm not so scared at night now. I just make sure that my ear is always covered with the blanket. I don't know why, but I can't stand having my ear sticking out when I sleep.

Anyway, this house is not nearly as spooky as Mouse's. Hers is much bigger and much older. They don't even use all the rooms upstairs. I asked Mouse if it scares her to live in a place like that. And she said she never thought about it. She has always lived in the same house and before that her mother's family lived in it, and some day she might get married and live there too. She said a long time ago Washington Irving slept in her house.

'Who's he?' I asked. 'Is he related to George?' I laughed at my own joke.

'You mean you don't know about Washington Irving?'

'No. I never even heard of him,' I told her.

'You mean you are going into fifth grade and you *still* never heard about Washington Irving?'

'I told you . . . no! Who is he anyway?'

'Well, I just can't believe it,' Mouse said. 'What's wrong with those schools in New York City?'

'If you know so much about him, why don't you tell me who he is at least?'

'Oh, I will, I will . . . I just can't believe that you don't already know, that's all,' Mouse said.

'Go on,' I told her. 'I'm listening.'

'Well . . . he was a very famous writer.'

'What did he write?' I asked.

'Oh, he wrote *Rip Van Winkle* and *The Legend of Sleepy Hollow.*'

'I've heard of Rip Van Winkle,' I said. 'He slept for a long time. But I've never heard about Sleepy Hollow.'

71

'You've never heard about Sleepy Hollow and Ichabod Crane?'

'That's right,' I said. 'You people in Tarrytown have a lot of useless information. If this Ichabod Crane was so important, I'd have heard about him in New York.'

'Well . . . all I can tell you is that the Headless Horseman rode right through here,' Mouse said, spreading her arms. 'Right through Tarrytown. So naturally it's important to us. How many towns do you think have a Headless Horseman riding through them?'

'What do you mean, *headless*?' I asked.

'Oh, he was this man on a horse and he had no head and Ichabod Crane saw him and got very scared.'

'But it's just a story, right? I mean, there's no such thing as a Headless Horseman!'

'Well . . .' Mouse said. 'It's kind of a story, but I believe it. In fact, I've heard him around

here lately. Haven't you?'

'Heard what?'

'The Headless Horseman! If you listen at night you can hear this eerie noise. And that's him – haunting Tarrytown.'

'I don't believe you,' I said.

'I don't care if you do or you don't. People who live in Tarrytown all year long know it's the truth!'

'What does he do?' I asked. 'Does he kill people?'

'Oh no! Nothing like that. He just rides around haunting. You know, like a ghost.'

'There's no such thing as ghosts,' I said.

'Maybe there is and maybe there isn't.'

I had a lot of trouble sleeping after Mouse told me that. I asked my father did he know about Ichabod Crane and the Headless Horseman and he said, 'Sure, it's a very famous story.'

73

'Do you believe it?' I asked.

'It's just a story, Sheila.'

'But there might be a Headless Horseman!'

'No, no. Washington Irving invented him.'

'But he lived around here, didn't he?'

'Yes, but so what?'

'Well,' I said, 'suppose he really saw this Headless Horseman and thought nobody would believe him, so instead he wrote a story about him. You see?'

'No, I don't see,' Daddy said. 'It's all made up. I'll bring you a book of his stories and you can read them. Then you'll understand.'

'No!' I shouted. 'I don't want to read about any Headless Horseman.'

After that, whenever I heard noises at night, I knew it was the Headless Horseman haunting Tarrytown. I wished it was September and we could go back to the city where there isn't room for any kind of horseman to go haunting at night.

8

Home Free

One grey, cloudy Saturday afternoon Mrs Ellis said she had to do some shopping. Mouse didn't want to go so her mother said she could stay at our house. Mouse gave me yo-yo lessons for half an hour, and all that time I wished there was something I could do better than Mouse and the other kids in Tarrytown. If only they had to live in the city for a month, I thought. Then I'd show them plenty! Probably not one of them could take a crosstown bus without getting lost!

When we got tired of yo-yoing Mouse said, 'Let's call the twins and see if they can come over.'

The twins are Sondra and Jane Van Arden. They swim at the pool too. They don't look

anything alike. Sondra is very shy and quiet and she always looks at your feet when you talk to her. They are both pretty good swimmers, but I have never seen Sondra dunk anyone. That's why I like her better than Jane.

When Mouse phoned them they said they would be right over because if they stayed home their mother was going to make them clean out their closets.

When they got to my house we had a snack of Oreos and milk. Sondra and Jane open their cookies and eat all the icing first. I used to do that but Libby said I was disgusting. When we were finished with our snack Mouse said, 'Want to play indoor hide-and-seek?'

'Hey, yeah,' Jane said. 'At your house, Mouse!'

'But we can't,' I said. 'Her mother isn't home.'

Mouse and Jane laughed then and Sondra said, 'There's a special way to get into the Mouse

House when her mother isn't home.'

'And just wait till you see it!' Jane said.

So we walked down the road to Mouse's and when we got there the girls showed me the milk door. It's a small door on the side of the house, near the kitchen. Mouse unlatched it and said, 'See, this is where the milkman puts our stuff. My mother never has to go outside to get it. Isn't that neat?'

'Yeah,' I said. 'It's really neat. It's kind of a built-in milk box!'

'Right!' Jane said. 'Only it's not a box, because it leads right into the house.'

Mouse boosted Jane up and Jane crawled through the milk door. Then Sondra boosted Mouse and she crawled through. I gave Sondra a boost and was wondering who would boost me when Sondra cried, 'Help . . . I'm stuck!'

'You can't be,' Mouse said.

'I am!' Sondra yelled. 'I really am!'

'You need to go on a diet!' Jane called from inside.

'Please do something!' Sondra begged.

Since I was the only one left on the outside I pulled Sondra's legs, trying to get her back out. When that didn't work, Jane and Mouse pulled from the inside, hoping to get her through the milk door. But nothing happened.

Sondra cried, 'I'm doomed! I'll be here forever.'

Jane said we should call the Fire Department and let them chop her out, but Mouse said her mother might get mad about that.

I could see that unless I took charge of the situation nothing would get done. So I said, 'Mouse, you and Jane open the regular door and help me on the outside.'

'I never thought of that,' Mouse said.

'You should have,' I told her. 'Because if you had been the only one to crawl through the

78

milk door in the first place, none of this would have happened. You could have unlocked the back door and we would have walked in like any other human beings.'

Mouse didn't answer me, but she and Jane did what I told them to and joined me on the outside. 'OK,' I said, 'now pull Sondra by the legs.'

All three of us pulled as hard as we could, but she still wouldn't budge. 'We need rope. Do you have any?' I asked Mouse.

'I think so,' she said. 'In the garage.'

'Well . . . don't just stand there. Go and get it!'

Mouse ran to the garage and came back with the rope. I tied it on to Sondra's ankles and we all pulled and pulled until we got her out. By that time she was crying for real and her ankles were full of rope burns.

'We've got to carry her inside now,' I said.

'I'll take her arms. Mouse, you take her legs and Jane, you grab her middle.'

As we were carrying her into the house Sondra kept screaming, 'Put me down! Put me down!' Some people don't know when other people are trying to help them!

We got her into the kitchen and put her down on the floor. Mouse said, 'Her legs are a mess. The bandages are upstairs. We better get her up there too.'

'That's crazy,' I said. 'You go and get the bandages and some first-aid cream and we'll fix her up down here.'

So Mouse ran upstairs and came back with a million little tubes and bottles and bandages and we all played doctor, fixing Sondra up. Of course I was the only one who knew just which medicine to put on each of Sondra's wounds. So I was really the main doctor and the others were my assistants.

80

We must have done a good job because Sondra stopped crying and said her legs felt much better. She even managed to walk up the stairs so we could start our game of hide-and-seek.

Mouse told Sondra she didn't have to be It because she had already suffered enough. The only rules to indoor hide-and-seek were, we had to stay upstairs and the attic was off limits. Home Base was the basin in the hall bathroom.

We did once-twice-three shoot to see who would be It first. I lost. I hate to be It, especially in a strange place. I always get this creepy feeling. And I've never played hide-and-seek inside before, except with Daddy, and that's not the same at all because nobody's going to pop out from under something and scare me.

But I closed my eyes and counted to seventy-five before I hollered, 'Ready or not . . . here I come!' I was supposed to count to one hundred,

but I'm sure nobody noticed. If they did I would just tell them I am a very fast counter.

The house was quiet, except for some squeaks now and then. I wanted to find the others in a hurry so I wouldn't be all alone. I walked from bedroom to bedroom but I didn't search under the beds or in the closets. I was afraid of what I might find. Suppose Washington Irving left something behind when he slept here a hundred years ago? I wonder if the Headless Horseman ever comes inside houses. If he does, I know he would choose this one, because it's so old he would feel at home. I went into Betsy's room. Ootch was on her bed. I made a lot of noise, hoping one of the others would hear me and laugh. But no one did. Just as I was coming out of Betsy's room Jane made a mad dash for the hall bathroom and yelled, 'Home-free-all!'

Now at least I had some company. I was glad she came out, even though I didn't catch her. I

had to concentrate on finding Mouse or Sondra. If they all got Home Free I would wind up as It again. Jane walked around with me and we found Sondra sitting in the bathroom in Mr and Mrs Ellis's bedroom. Now all we needed was Mouse. We looked and looked but we couldn't find her.

Finally Jane said, 'Do you suppose she's in the laundry chute again?'

'No,' Sondra said. 'She got in awful trouble the last time. Remember . . .'

'What laundry chute?' I asked.

'Oh, it's this hole in the wall where Mrs Ellis drops the dirty clothes. They fall down to the basement, where she does the wash. Come on, let's look,' Jane said.

We walked down the long hallway to the attic door. Next to it was a smaller door that looked like an oven. Jane pulled it open and looked inside. 'No Mouse,' she said.

'How did she hide in there? Didn't she fall down to the basement?' I asked.

'Oh . . . she can really hang on,' Jane said.

'But the last time her mother caught her and she got it good!' Sondra told me.

'Where do you suppose she is?' I asked.

'Who knows?' Jane said.

Just then we all heard a scary noise.

Whooo whooo whooo

All three of us grabbed hold of each other and Sondra started laughing like crazy. Then Jane started. So I laughed as loud as they did. Even louder, to show I thought it was funny too.

Whooo whooo whooo

Jane pulled away and flung open the attic door.

Mouse shouted, 'BOO!' and jumped out at us. 'Ha ha . . . I really scared you!'

'Scared who?' I asked. 'You think a little noise like that could scare us?'

'Yeah,' Sondra said, 'we all knew it was you.'

'And besides that,' I told Mouse, 'you broke the rules. The attic is supposed to be off limits! You said so yourself.'

'Yeah,' Sondra and Jane said together.

I didn't want to play any more hide-and-seek after that, but Mouse promised not to scare us again. She said she'd even be It just to show what a good sport she was. So Sondra, Jane and me hid while Mouse stood at the basin and counted up to one hundred – no cheating allowed.

I ran to Mrs Ellis's room and hid inside her closet. My heart was thumping so loud I thought it might explode and that would be the end of me. I crouched in the corner and waited. I never know when to run for Home Base. Other kids get Home Free. Why don't I? I sat still for a long time. Why didn't Mouse come? Should

I try for Home Base? I heard footsteps. So, she was finally going to have a look in her mother's room, I thought. It's about time.

The footsteps came closer and closer. I hid behind a long bathrobe. Maybe she wouldn't find me after all, and as soon as she was gone I could run for Home Base.

The closet door opened. I peeked out from behind the robe. All I saw were feet. They didn't belong to Mouse. They were much too big.

Whoever it was started moving the clothes around. The robe I was hiding behind wiggled, and then there was a terrible scream. I think it came from me!

'Sheila Tubman!' Mrs Ellis shouted. 'You nearly scared me to death!'

I tried to say something but I couldn't make the words come out. I was shaking. Mrs Ellis reached down and helped me up. 'Come out

of there,' she said. 'What are you doing in my closet?'

'I don't know,' I told her.

'You better know. I'm waiting to hear your answer.'

'Well . . . you see . . .' I began.

And then Mouse, Sondra and Jane came into the room. 'Hi, Mom,' Mouse said.

'Mouse! What is going on here?' Mrs Ellis asked.

'We were playing a little hide-and-seek,' Mouse said.

'You are supposed to be at Sheila's house,' her mother said. 'Mrs Tubman is going crazy trying to find you.'

'No kidding,' Mouse said.

'That's right!' Mrs Ellis turned to me. 'Sheila, go and phone your mother right now and tell her where you are.'

*

That night Mr Ellis boarded up the milk door and Mrs Ellis put out a regular milk box. And we all knew that was the end of indoor hide-and-seek at the Mouse House.

9
Babar Strikes Again

After three weeks of day camp my favourite activity is still pottery. Mouse, Russ Bindel and Sam Sweeney agree. The four of us haven't switched activities yet, even though we are supposed to try something new every week. Denise says by the end of the summer we should each have a really good bowl to take home with us. My mother is not as happy about pottery as I am. This is because I come home covered with clay every day. It even gets in my hair and ears. The only bad things about pottery are I have to put up with a lot of shampoos and Mom is always chasing me with the Q-Tips.

Russ Bindel's mother runs the camp office. She's pretty nice. Russ looks just like her. He's a

year older than me, but so small he looks about eight. And between Russ and his mother I have never seen so many freckles.

Sam Sweeney reminds me of Peter Hatcher. He thinks he knows everything. And when his clay elephant broke in the kiln he blamed it on me and Mouse for making too much noise while it was baking. Denise told him it wasn't anybody's fault. And maybe he left too many cracks in his elephant because besides breaking in half one tusk also fell off. Sam is the only one of us who doesn't use the pottery wheel. He's always making animals, and elephants are his favourite. I can't imagine what he does with all his elephants. Mouse and I call him Babar in private.

Of course we can't stay at pottery all day. That's our main activity, from 9.30 until lunchtime. After lunch we are supposed to have a quiet hour. We usually break up into

small groups and sit under the trees. Most of our counsellors play the guitar and we sing a lot. I have learned some very unusual songs at day camp. One is about Anne Boleyn, who was married to King Henry the Eighth of England. But when she didn't have any boy babies he decided she should have her head chopped off. And in this song she is back haunting King Henry's castle, 'with her head tucked underneath her arm'. I like to sing the song but I don't like to think about her walking around like that. She reminds me of the Headless Horseman.

This morning Denise asked me to go to the camp office to tell Mrs Bindel that she is expecting an important phone call. Mrs Bindel was running some papers off on a very old-fashioned machine.

'Don't you have a photocopier?' I asked.

'No,' Mrs Bindel said.

'We have one in school. How come you don't have one here?'

'They're very expensive. We make do with this old mimeograph.'

'Isn't it hard work to crank out all those copies?'

'No,' Mrs Bindel said.

I watched her for a while. 'Want me to help you?' I asked.

'That's very nice of you, Sheila. But you'd better get back to your activity. And tell Denise I'll come and get her when her phone call comes through.'

I still didn't go. Because all of a sudden I had the greatest idea of how to show the Tarrytown kids that I *was* an expert at something besides bandaging legs.

'We had a class newspaper last year,' I told Mrs Bindel. 'I used to run off the copies in the office. Nobody had to help me. I did it all by myself.'

'That must have been very interesting,' Mrs Bindel said.

'It was. I could use your old machine if we had a camp newspaper, couldn't I?'

'Well, I suppose so. But we don't have a camp newspaper.'

'We should,' I said.

'But we don't,' Mrs Bindel told me.

'Maybe we will!' I called, running out of the office.

I ran right into Mr Healstrom, the director of our camp. He caught me so I didn't fall down. 'What's your hurry?' he asked.

'Oh, Mr Healstrom! You're just the one I want to see,' I told him. 'Do you know what we need here?'

'No, what?'

'A newspaper. A camp newspaper! And I've decided it's my duty to start one.'

Mr Healstrom said, 'That's a very good idea.'

'I knew you'd think so. I'll be in charge of everything,' I said. 'And I'll run off the copies on the mimeograph machine in the office. Even though it's old-fashioned I know I can work it.'

'You may need some help, Sheila. Suppose I let you announce your plans this afternoon. Then you can form committees and get started.'

'I don't need committees,' I said. 'I'm very experienced. I know exactly what to do!'

'Running a newspaper is a big job, Sheila,' Mr Healstrom said. 'And nobody does it alone.'

'I can do it, Mr Healstrom. You'll see. I've even got a name picked out.'

'What is it?' he asked.

'It's a surprise. You'll find out next Friday when you read the first issue.'

'Well . . .' Mr Healstrom said, 'you seem determined to try it on your own. So, good luck!'

'Oh thanks, Mr Healstrom! Thanks a lot!'

I ran back to pottery and told everyone

about our camp newspaper.

'When's it coming out?' Mouse asked.

'On Friday,' I said. 'And I'm going to be very busy between now and then. I may have to skip pottery. You know, it's a big job to put out a paper all by yourself.'

'That's just what I was thinking,' Denise said. 'What you need is a committee. Maybe you could get a reporter from each group to tell you what's going on.'

'I'll help you,' Mouse said. 'I'd like to be a reporter.'

'I don't need any reporters,' I told everyone. 'I can do all that myself.'

'But if I'm a reporter we can work together,' Mouse said. 'We can be a team.'

'It's *my* idea and *I'm* doing everything!' I told her.

'Well, if that's the way you want to be about it,' Mouse said. I could tell that Mouse was

wishing she had thought up the idea of having a camp newspaper. And Russ and Sam were really surprised that I knew so much about it.

'Is my mother going to type the newspaper for you?' Russ asked.

'Of course not,' I told him. 'I'll type it myself.'

'You know how to type?' he asked.

'There's nothing to it!' I said.

That night I wrote my first story. I called it 'Babar Strikes Again'. It was all about Sam Sweeney and his clay elephants, but of course I never mentioned him by name.

Starting the next morning I made my rounds of all the activities. I carried my pad around with me and kept a pencil tucked behind my ear. I jotted down all kinds of interesting things and story ideas such as 'Libby the Dancing Skeleton' and 'The Real Reason Denise Goes Barefoot'. I discovered that at lunch. I was crawling around listening to bits of conversation when I noticed

the bottoms of Denise's feet. She was sitting on the grass, leaning against a tree, and the bottoms of her feet pointed up. I don't know how I ever missed seeing them before. They are covered with warts! No wonder she doesn't wear shoes.

The next day was very hot, and as I trudged around from activity to activity I wondered what Mouse, Russ and Sam were doing at pottery. I didn't come up with any new story ideas so I wrote a weather report, arranged a list of Dos and Don'ts about the camp bus, and made up a crossword puzzle of counsellors' names. I offered a prize to the first person to hand it in with all the right names.

On Thursday I went to the office to type out the first edition of my camp newspaper. I figured it would only take a few minutes and then I could go back to pottery. I was starting to miss Mouse and my regular camp routine.

Mouse and Russ were probably having a lot of fun with the pottery wheel, and with me out of the way they'd each have extra turns.

But after typing for the longest time I was still working on 'Babar Strikes Again' and the wastebasket was full of my mistakes. Finally Mrs Bindel told me she really had to use her typewriter and I had better handwrite my newspaper on the stencil. I said that was fine with me because everyone in New York knows I have the best handwriting in the whole fourth grade.

I found out pretty fast that it's not so easy to write your best on a stencil. I kept goofing. And none of my lines came out straight. They all ran downhill. I threw away the first two stencils and made up my mind that the third one would be it, no matter what!

Across the whole top of the page I printed:

NEWSDATE
by Sheila the Great

That looked really neat except it took up a lot of room, so by the time I got to my crossword puzzle on the bottom of the page, I had to make it very small. I think I spelled 'counsellor' wrong, but you can't erase when you're using a stencil so I had to leave it that way. By the time I finished drawing little pictures of all our activities along the side margins of my newspaper, it was time to go home. And was I glad!

On Friday morning I was ready to use the mimeograph machine. I thought I'd zip out the seventy-five copies I needed and still make it back to pottery. Denise would probably let me use the wheel the whole time because I haven't had a turn all week.

But I discovered that you can't just zip out copies on an old mimeograph machine. For

one thing, the machine uses a special kind of ink. And after half an hour my hands were full of it but the machine didn't have enough because every page came out blank. So I poured in a ton of ink and then when I cranked out the first few copies big blobs of purple were all over the paper and you couldn't read anything I'd written.

That's when Mrs Bindel said she would get the machine going for me. I told her, 'What this camp needs is a good photocopier.'

'You'll be more experienced next week, Sheila. It probably won't take so long then.'

I didn't want to think about next week or the week after that, or spending the rest of the summer putting out the camp newspaper.

Two hours later I was still cranking out copies. They looked better than the first batch, which I had to throw away. This time you could read practically everything. But

the pictures in the margins weren't too clear. Still, if you looked hard you could see that they were pictures. I couldn't understand why the crossword puzzle came out with such wavy lines though. But at least I had my seventy-five copies of NEWSDATE ready. I didn't much care how they looked any more. I was so glad to be done!

I took my seventy-five copies, yelled goodbye to Mrs Bindel, and ran out of the office. I personally handed a copy of my newspaper to every kid in camp.

When Mouse saw it she said, 'What kind of newspaper is this?'

And I said, 'What do you mean by that?'

She said, 'I never heard of a newspaper that's handwritten. It doesn't even look like a newspaper to me.'

'Well, that's how much you know!' I told her. 'Anybody can type out a newspaper. It takes

special talent and a lot more work to handwrite one!'

'What are these funny smudges up and down the sides of the paper?'

'Funny smudges! You must need glasses. Anyone with eyes can see they're pictures of our camp activities!'

'No kidding!' Mouse said, looking closer. 'All I see are ink blots.'

'You better have your eyes examined,' I told her. 'Everyone else in camp knows that they are pictures.'

That's when Russ came up to me and said, 'Hey, Sheila . . . why didn't you get my mother to help you with the mimeograph? Then you wouldn't have gotten your papers all smudged up.'

Before I had a chance to say anything two big boys walked over to us and handed me the finished crossword puzzle.

'OK, Sheila the Great,' one of them said. 'What's the big prize?'

That's when I realized I didn't have a prize to give. I was so sure nobody would be able to figure out my puzzle!

'Well . . .' the other boy said.

I had to think fast. How would it look if SHEILA THE GREAT didn't have a super prize to give? 'Congratulations!' I said. 'You are both very lucky. Very lucky. Very, very lucky!'

'So what do we win?' they asked.

'You win the camp newspaper! That's what you win! Next week you get to run it all by yourself! Unless, of course, you feel you need a committee. Most people aren't able to run newspapers by themselves.'

'Some prize!'

'I knew you'd think so,' I told them, smiling at Mouse and Russ.

*

That night I made up my mind that the next time I think up such a great project I will be the boss and my committee of workers will do everything else!

10
Jennifer's Friend

It turned out that Allen and Paul, the boys who won my contest, liked being in charge of the camp newspaper. They formed all kinds of committees and hardly missed any of their regular activities. Mrs Bindel volunteered to do all their typing. Some people really take the easy way out! They even changed the name of my paper from NEWSDATE BY SHEILA THE GREAT, to *Allen and Paul . . . Tell All*.

Mouse is one of the camp reporters. She acts like that's a big deal.

'You must really like newspaper work if you gave up after just one week,' Mouse said.

'It's not that I don't like it,' I told her. 'It's just that the challenge was gone.'

'Well,' Mouse said, 'I think it's a challenge *every* week and I've decided that I'm going to be a real reporter some day. And I'm going to have a byline too! So when you see "By Mouse Ellis" in your paper you can tell your friends you knew me when I was starting out.'

'Swell,' I said. 'You do that. I will probably be something more exciting myself.'

'Like what?' Mouse asked.

'Oh . . . something!'

'You can't tell me because you don't know. Right?'

'I'm still deciding,' I said. 'I might be a weather forecaster.'

'A weather forecaster?'

'Yes. I think it would be pretty exciting to always know the weather in advance.'

'Hey,' Mouse said. 'I just got a swell idea. Maybe I can be a reporter on TV and you can be the weather forecaster and we'll call our

show *Ellis and Tubman Report*.'

'I like *Tubman and Ellis Report* better,' I said.

'Maybe it should be *Mouse and Sheila Report*.'

'Or *Sheila and Mouse Report*,' I said.

'Well, we don't have to decide about that now.'

'Right. It's the show that's the good idea,' I said. 'What we call it isn't that important.'

'But we'll definitely be a team,' Mouse said.

'Of course we will,' I told her.

'Let's shake on it.'

'OK,' I said. We shook hands hard.

One reason I want to be a weather forecaster is that I will always know in advance if there's going to be a thunderstorm and I will have time to prepare myself. Last night there was an awful storm. My mother and father don't know this, but I sat in my closet until it was over.

This afternoon, when I got home from camp, I turned on the radio. I sat next to it until I heard the weather report. Tonight is supposed to be clear and cool. That's good. That means there's nothing for me to worry about.

I fell asleep with no trouble. But in the middle of the night I woke up. There was a terrible racket outside. It wasn't thunder but it sounded pretty scary anyway. At first I put my pillow over my head, hoping the noise would go away. But it didn't.

When I couldn't stand it any more I jumped out of bed and ran to my window. And what did I see? Two Jennifers! As if one isn't bad enough! And both of them baying at the moon at the same time.

The next morning at breakfast I told the whole family about Jennifer's friend. Everyone seemed to think it was very funny. Everyone except me!

Two days later Libby reported that Jennifer's friend is definitely a boy dog. 'How do you know?' I asked.

'I saw him make,' Libby said. 'He used the big tree in the backyard, near the fence.'

'I'm not surprised,' Daddy said.

Jennifer's friend comes to visit every night now. It is getting harder and harder to sleep in this house. In the morning Jennifer's friend is gone. We don't know who he belongs to.

I don't like leaving the house these days. I know it isn't safe. I told my mother, 'Jennifer's friend just runs around loose. You can't expect me to go outside with that dog around here.'

'He only comes at night,' Mom said.

'That's what you *think*,' I told her. 'But you can't be sure, can you?'

'No,' Mom said. 'I can't be sure. But there is nothing for you to worry about. Jennifer's

friend is perfectly harmless.'

'Oh he is, is he! Did he tell you that? Did he ring the bell and say, *Hello Mrs Tubman. I'm perfectly harmless!'*

My mother sighed. 'I can see there's no point in discussing it with you. Your mind is already made up.'

A few days later Mouse was over. We were yo-yoing in the driveway. Mouse has a new Duncan Butterfly. A Butterfly is a regular yo-yo put together backwards, so the flat ends are on the outside. Nobody told me this. I figured it out myself. Mouse was trying to teach me a new yo-yo trick called 'Round the World, but I kept missing and hitting myself in the head.

All of a sudden I had the feeling I was being watched. I turned around slowly and there he was – Jennifer's friend! I screamed and threw my yo-yo at him. He came after me. I ran as fast as I could – right into the yard where Jennifer was

tied up. Her friend was barking like crazy and I could tell he was already thinking about how I would taste so I kept running and screaming until I tripped over Jennifer's chain. I fell down and was sure that was the end of me. So I closed my eyes and cried. When I felt my legs were wet all over I knew the blood was pouring out of them.

In a minute my mother was bending over me and I heard Mouse say, 'She just went crazy, Mrs Tubman. I couldn't even stop her!'

'My legs . . . my legs . . .' I cried. 'Do something, stop the blood.'

'What blood?' Mom asked. 'There's no blood.'

'But they're all wet,' I sobbed. 'I can feel how wet they are.'

'Open your eyes, Sheila,' Mom said. 'And you'll see why.'

I opened one eye and then the other. I rolled over and Mom helped me sit up. Jennifer, that

dumb old dog, was licking my legs!

'I'm going to get awful hives,' I told Mouse. 'Just awful! They'll probably be as big as apples.'

Mouse didn't say anything. She just looked at me and shook her head.

Later, Mom took me to the doctor because when I tripped over Jennifer's chain I scraped my leg. I said, 'I told you, didn't I? I told you it wasn't safe to keep that dog around here. Just see what she's done to me . . . just see!'

'Jennifer and her friend did not do anything to you, Sheila,' Mom said. 'And if you had just kept calm nothing would have happened at all.'

'I was calm!' I said. 'Jennifer's friend is the one who got all excited. And did you see the size of his teeth?'

Mouse came over after supper. 'I wanted to make sure you were OK,' she said.

'I'm fine,' I told her.

'Did you get hives?'

'Hives?'

'Yes, from Jennifer licking you.'

'Oh . . . yes, I got awful hives,' I said. 'All over my liver and intestines.'

'Your liver and intestines?'

'Yes. And the doctor said I was really lucky this time. I didn't get any on my lungs. They're the worst kind.'

Mouse tilted her head and didn't say anything for a minute. So neither did I. Finally she looked me right in the eye. 'Sheila, if a person is scared of something a person should just admit it. Don't you think so?'

'Oh, definitely!' I said. 'And if I was ever afraid of anything I'd be the first to admit it.'

'Me too,' Mouse said. 'Did I ever tell you I'm scared of dragonflies?'

'You are?'

'Yes. Even though I know they can't hurt me I'm very scared of them. How about you? What makes you afraid?'

'Oh . . . uh . . . let me think . . .'

'Take your time,' Mouse said.

'You know,' I told her, 'I really can't think of anything I'm scared of except maybe lions.'

'Lions?'

'Yes. You know . . . lions!'

'And that's it?' Mouse asked.

'Yes. I just can't think of another thing.'

Mouse tilted her head to the other side. Was she trying to get a different view of me?

'It's getting dark,' I told her. 'Remember, your mother doesn't like you walking around in the dark.'

'I'm going,' Mouse said. 'See you tomorrow, Sheila. I hope you don't run into any lions!'

'Ha ha,' I called.

*

114

Soon after that Jennifer's friend stopped coming to visit and Jennifer made unhappy noises at night. She refused to eat. Daddy got worried and took her to the vet. And that's how we found out Jennifer is going to be a mother.

Daddy wrote to the Egrans, telling them about Jennifer. They wrote back.

Dear Buzz, Jean, and girls,

We are enjoying England although the boys miss home and Jennifer. We are all thrilled to hear the good news. Imagine our little Jennifer a mother! Thank goodness we'll be home for the big event. Of course you get the pick of the litter. I know having a puppy will make the girls very happy, especially since they are taking care of Jennifer this summer. We are glad to hear that you are comfortable in our house and

that the girls like Tarrytown. See you
in September.

Sally, George, and the boys

PS Bobby wants to add something . . .

My mother says that a girl named
Sheila is in my room. Did she find my
note? Tell her this - Just remember, I
meant what I said! I'm bringing home
21 new models to add to my collection.
Everything better be just the way I left
it!

B. E.

The whole letter made me mad. Especially the
part about the pick of the litter. Who said we
want one of Jennifer's puppies anyway? Don't
the Egrans know that dogs are very unhappy in
the city? They have to be indoors all the time.
There aren't any backyards where they can be
tied up. For a professor, George Egran isn't very

smart, or he would know better than to offer us one of his dumb old dogs.

Libby didn't agree. 'I just can't wait!' she said. I'm going to pick him out myself. And I'm going to be in charge of him and he's going to sleep on my bed and I am going to be the happiest girl who ever lived!'

'You better quit thinking about having a puppy,' I told her. 'Because you can't.'

'Since when are important decisions left up to you?' Libby asked.

'You think you're going to bring some puppy into our room to sleep on your bed? You're really crazy. You know I'm allergic to dogs! You know I get giant hives inside me!'

'The little spoiled brat isn't going to get her own way this time!' Libby screamed. 'This time the spoiled brat is going to have to learn that I count too. I am also a member of this family.'

'Girls . . . girls . . .' Daddy said.

'Tell her, Father. Tell her you're going to let me have one of Jennifer's puppies.'

'Oh, Daddy . . . you wouldn't. You wouldn't do that to me,' I cried.

'Jennifer isn't even having her puppies until September. There's no point in discussing it now,' Daddy said.

'If I don't get one I'm leaving home!' Libby said.

'And if she *does* get one *I'm* leaving home!' I told everyone.

'In about one minute I think *I'm* going to leave home!' Mom said.

'That's a good idea,' Daddy said. 'Let's you and me run off and leave *them* together.'

'Very funny,' Libby said.

'Yeah . . . very funny,' I added.

'The discussion is closed for now,' Daddy told us. 'Your mother and I will make the decision when the time comes.'

Libby ran out of the room and up the stairs. I heard her door slam. I picked up the Egrans's letter and went up to my room, but I didn't slam the door. I flopped on to my bed and read the PS from Bobby again. I decided to write back.

Dear B. E.

Sure I found your note. And your 27 bottles of paint AND your 6 tubes of Testor's glue. And if you think I am using all that junk you are sick. Me and Mouse (who is my best friend) couldn't care less about your dumb old models. So ha ha! And your dog Jennifer makes too much noise at night!

Yours untruly,
Sunny Tubman
Otherwise known as
SHEILA THE GREAT

11
Never-Never Land

Libby spends most of her free time with Jennifer. She is studying books on how to deliver babies. Even though the vet says Jennifer's puppies won't be born until September, when the Egrans are back, Libby says it can't hurt to be prepared.

'Jennifer should sleep inside at night,' Libby announced at supper.

'Oh no!' I said.

'She can sleep on my bed,' Libby said. 'Oh please, Father! She needs to be where it's warm. Don't you understand?'

'I'll ask the vet,' Daddy said. 'But I think it's all right for her to stay in her doghouse as long as the weather is warm.'

'If it isn't all right for her to stay out there I'm

leaving,' I said. 'A deal's a deal!'

'Selfish, selfish, selfish person!' Libby said, giving me a kick under the table.

Lucky for me the vet told Daddy it is fine for Jennifer to stay in her doghouse for the rest of the summer.

When she isn't learning to be a dog doctor, Libby is practising how to sing. She wants to play the part of Wendy in the camp production of *Peter Pan*. Libby's singing makes her dancing look great. I never knew my sister has such an awful voice. I have to hold my ears when she starts in with her songs. I know she will never get the part of Wendy.

Mouse and I are not trying out for parts in the play. We signed up to paint scenery instead. So did Sam Sweeney. He has already painted four elephants. Since when are there elephants in Never-Never Land? Russ wants to play Captain

Hook. But if you ask me he looks more like Peter Pan.

On Tuesday Libby didn't eat any breakfast. She said she was too nervous about trying out for the play. 'I just have to be Wendy, or I'll die,' she told us.

On Tuesday night she didn't eat any supper. That's because she didn't get the part of Wendy. I knew she wouldn't. I didn't think she should be acting so disappointed. She got a very important part in the play. She is going to be Captain Hook.

I told her, 'You're lucky, Libby. Russ would give anything to be Captain Hook.'

'Well, let him!' Libby cried. 'I don't want to play the part of some disgusting old man!'

'He can't,' I said. 'He's going to be Peter Pan.'

This news made Libby cry even harder.

Daddy told Libby to get into the spirit of the play and accept her part. After all, she could be

painting scenery like me and Mouse.

The next day Libby spent hours and hours in the bathroom looking at herself. I know, because every time I had to use it she was in there. So finally I got tired of knocking and I just walked right in on her.

She didn't even yell at me. She just said, 'I am so ugly it's unbelievable!'

'Oh, you're not that bad,' I said.

'How would you know?' Libby asked. 'You look just like me!'

'I do?'

'Of course,' she said. 'Just look in the mirror.'

I looked. 'I don't know, Libby,' I said. 'I don't think I look like you.'

'Well, you do!' Libby screamed. 'And just wait until you're thirteen. You'll be as ugly as me if not uglier! Oh . . . I could just cry!'

'You've been crying for three days already,' I reminded her.

'Oh, shut up!'

I went down to the kitchen and told my mother what Libby said.

'Libby is just feeling bad about not getting the part of Wendy in the play. She'll get over it,' Mom said.

'She thinks she didn't get it because she's ugly.'

'She's making excuses. And she's feeling ugly. Looks are all a matter of how you feel, you know. If you feel beautiful you are beautiful! It all comes from inside.'

'No kidding!' I said. 'I never knew that.'

Mom smiled.

'Why don't you tell that to Libby?' I asked.

'I tried,' Mom said. 'But she wouldn't listen. Here, have a carrot.'

'Thanks,' I said, taking it. I think I could live on raw carrots. They are the best-tasting food in the whole world.

That afternoon I went to the pool with Mouse and Betsy. Mom said she would stay home with Libby and try to cheer her up.

'Do you think I'm ugly?' I asked Mouse.

Betsy answered, 'Yes. But I love you just the same. And so does Ootch.'

'Oh, Betsy!' Mouse said. 'Sheila's not ugly and you know it.'

'OK,' Betsy said. 'You're not ugly.'

'Libby says I am,' I told Mouse. 'She says I look just like her and that she is one of the ugliest people on earth!'

'She's stupid!' Mouse said.

'I know that . . . but do you think she knows what she's talking about when she says I'll look just like her some day?'

'Definitely not,' Mouse told me.

I was happy to hear that.

The next day Libby decided to learn every

part in the play. She says this is just in case someone gets sick at the last minute and she has to play another part – like maybe Wendy!

I asked her if she plays Wendy, then who will be Captain Hook, and she says I am very dumb to even ask such a question. I don't understand Libby at all.

Me and Mouse have finished painting six huge trees and now we are starting on the archway. When Wendy and the other kids walk through it that means they are in Never-Never Land. They aren't going to fly across the stage like they're supposed to. They're just going to pretend by flapping their arms.

The problem is the archway won't stand up by itself. Every time we put it on the stage it falls to one side. So Mike, the counsellor in charge of scenery, says that me and Mouse are going to have to stand behind it and hold it up while the play is going on. Mouse doesn't want to. She

says she's too embarrassed. But I think it will be great fun to be on the stage holding up such an important piece of scenery.

All of our parents are invited to the play, plus anyone else who wants to come. Daddy is tacking a note about the production on the bulletin board at college. He is sure some of his students will want to see the show.

The girl who is playing the part of Wendy is Maryann Markman. I think her name is very good for an actress. It sounds better than Libby Tubman. I wonder why my mother and father didn't think of that when they named my sister. Sheila Tubman doesn't sound much better, but at least I don't want to be a famous actress or ballerina. And, anyway, I could always call myself Sunny Tub or something like that.

The one thing I have noticed about Maryann Markman is that when she's rehearsing she sings very nice and loud and is pretty good at

her part. But as soon as anyone who isn't in the play sits down to watch she sings so soft you can hardly hear her. I wonder what will happen the night of the play.

Libby is still hoping Maryann will get sick and that she will have to play the part of Wendy. Since I'm always on the stage holding up the scenery I'm learning all the parts too. That way, if Libby winds up playing Wendy, maybe I can be Captain Hook.

Finally the night of the play came. Daddy gave Libby a rose in honour of the occasion. 'Oh, Father!' Libby cried. 'You are too thoughtful!'

I'm glad this play will be over tonight. I'm sick of my sister, the actress.

Me and Mouse had to dress in blue and yellow so we would blend into the rest of the scenery in case either one of us shows through.

Maryann Markman got there in plenty of

128

time and she wasn't sneezing or coughing or acting sick. Libby looked stupid in her Captain Hook suit. But Russ was a perfect Peter Pan. It's too bad he can't *really* fly.

Everybody did fine during the first act except Mouse coughed once, when Russ was singing. He stopped right in the middle of his song and waited for her to finish. Maryann's voice was low but very sweet. When she ran through the archway she almost knocked me over. But I hung on and the archway stayed up.

Libby came on in the middle of the second act. She sang her song very loud and when she was done the audience clapped for her. I guess sometimes it is better to sing loud and be heard than to sing very nicely like Maryann, who nobody could hear but me and Mouse. Hearing Libby sing so loud seemed to make Maryann forget her lines, because she just stood there and didn't say anything. Finally, I whispered her next line to help her remember. When she still didn't say anything I said her lines for her. I don't know if the audience noticed this or not, because Maryann did move her lips. I said her lines for her all during that act. Libby looked over at me once and made a terrible face, but Maryann needed me. What else could I do? Mouse was laughing all this time and neither one of us remembered about holding up the archway. So the next time Russ ran through, it fell to the side.

But I don't think we ruined the play, like Libby says, because we managed to get it up again in just a few seconds. All in all I think it was a very successful show even though Libby says she is never speaking to me again.

12
Blowing Bubbles

I am down to three swimming lessons a week. Marty says I am ready to learn to put my face in the water because there is nothing else he can teach me until I do. I told him, 'I can't put my face in the water and there's a very good reason why I can't, which you don't even know about!'

'I'm listening,' Marty said. 'What's your reason?'

'Something very important that you probably never even considered.'

'Well . . .'

'You really want to know my reason?'

'I'm waiting,' Marty said.

'OK. I'll tell you. The reason I cannot possibly

put my face in the water of this pool is that I am scared!'

'Sheila!' Marty practically shouted. 'I'm proud of you!'

'You are?'

'Yes. Do you realize this is the first time you've been honest with me?' Marty asked.

'It is?'

'Yes, it is. You've finally admitted it . . . you're scared. That's the first step in the right direction. From now on everything will be a snap!' Marty jumped into the pool. 'Come on, Sheila. I want to show you something.'

I walked down the steps and stood next to him.

'Watch this,' Marty said, putting his face in the water. Big bubbles came to the surface. He turned his head to the side and took a breath. Then he stuck it back in and blew some more bubbles. He did that ten times. He made it look easy.

When he was done I clapped my hands. 'That was very good, Marty,' I said.

'OK, wise guy. Now let's see you do it.'

'I can't,' I said. 'I'm too scared.'

'I'll hold your hand.'

I looked at Marty and thought about what my mother told me. That if I can't swim with my face in the water by the end of the summer Marty will give back all the money from my swimming lessons. I hate to think of Marty having a hard time because of me. But he never should have made such a silly deal with Mom.

'Please, Sheila,' Marty said. 'Give it a try.'

'Oh, all right,' I said, grabbing Marty's hand. I put my face down into the water. I nearly choked to death! Marty had to whack me on the back until I stopped coughing.

'What were you supposed to do, Sheila?' he asked.

'I was supposed to blow bubbles,' I answered.

'And did you?'

'No, I breathed regular.'

'And what did you find out?'

'That I can't breathe regular in the water.'

'That's right!' Marty said. 'So let's try it again. And this time take a breath first and *then* blow it out.'

'OK.' I took a breath, but I started to laugh. Sometimes I do that when I'm really scared. And nothing stops me from laughing. Nothing! I laugh until my side feels as if it is going to split open. Usually I wind up with bad hiccups.

'Sheila . . . Sheila . . .' Marty said. 'What am I going to do with you? You're impossible!'

'I told you I was, didn't I?' I giggled.

'I should have believed you,' Marty said. 'Calm down now. Let's get to work.'

'I'm calm, I'm calm,' I told him. I took a big breath and put my face into the water. I think Marty was yelling something at me but I don't

know what. When I felt ready to explode I lifted my face and said, 'Well, how was that?'

'You forgot to let it out, Sheila.'

'Let what out?'

'The air . . . you took a big breath but then you didn't let it out.'

'Oh.' I knew something was wrong. I took a bigger breath, put my face in the water, and blew out. I made bubbles. Just like Marty!

I lifted my head and smiled.

'That's it!' Marty shouted. 'You did it . . . you really did it!'

'I did, didn't I?' I could hardly believe it myself. 'I really did do it!'

'Yes, and now I want you to try it ten times in a row.'

'Oh, Marty . . . do I have to? Isn't just once enough?'

Marty shook his head.

I took a breath and did what he told me to. I

blew very nice bubbles. Then I turned my head to the side, took another breath, and put my face back into the water. I did this four times before I forgot to blow the air out. That time I think I breathed in while my face was under the water. I wound up with a mouthful. When I stopped coughing I gasped, 'No more. Please . . . no more. Don't make me do it again.' I climbed out of the pool and ran for a towel. The chlorine really stings my eyes.

Marty followed me. 'OK, Sheila. That's it for today. But I want you to practise swimming with your face in the water. I'm going to give you the Beginner's Swimming Test before the end of the summer. I think you'll be able to pass it.'

'Me? Me pass a swimming test?' I asked.

'Yes . . . you!'

I always knew Marty was sick!

13
Slam Books

I'm going to have a slumber party. I've never had one. How could I when I have shared a room with Libby all my life? I just can't wait until Saturday night. Mouse, Sondra and Jane are coming, and Mom says we can all sleep in my room if my friends bring sleeping bags with them. I even have new pyjamas to wear. They are red-and-white striped. Mouse has the same ones. She promised to wear them so we can be twins like Sondra and Jane. My slumber party is going to be the best slumber party that ever was!

Since I have been planning everything so carefully I got really sore at Libby this morning when she told Mom, 'I'm going to invite

Maryann Markman to sleep over Saturday night.'

'Oh no!' I said. 'You know I'm having a slumber party.'

'So?' Libby asked. 'Who wants to get in your way?'

'That's not fair!' I said to Mom. 'Can't I do something just once without her butting in?'

'There's plenty of room, Sheila,' Mom said. 'If Libby wants Maryann to spend the night, there's no reason why she can't. It has nothing to do with you.'

'They'll try to boss us around,' I cried. 'Just like always.'

'Ha!' Libby said.

'Nobody's going to spoil your party,' Mom told me. 'I promise.'

'I don't see why *she* can't spend the night at Maryann's house instead,' I said.

'Because Maryann's parents are going

out and her mother doesn't want us to stay alone,' Libby said. 'Otherwise I would . . . in a second!'

I just know they will ruin everything!

On Saturday Maryann ate supper with us so she was already there when my friends rang the bell. But she and my sister were locked up in Libby's room listening to records and I hoped that's where they would stay for the rest of the night.

After Mouse, Sondra and Jane said hello to Daddy and Mom I took them up to my room and we spread out their sleeping bags. Sondra's and Jane's are the same. There is a picture of Snoopy on the front, zippers down the sides, and red flannel linings. Mouse brought a regular sleeping bag. The kind you use when you go camping. She said the last time she slept outside she woke up with a frog inside her bag. But since she likes frogs she didn't mind. I would much rather sleep in a sleeping bag indoors than out.

We arranged the sleeping bags on the floor next to my bed, with Mouse between Sondra and Jane. Then we showed each other our pyjamas and discussed the kind of toothpaste we use. Sondra and Jane didn't bring matching pyjamas, so me and Mouse turned out to be twins by ourselves.

Next, we got undressed and ready for bed, even though we didn't plan to go to sleep for hours and hours and maybe not even all night. Sondra changed her clothes in my closet. I think she is getting fatter. But I wouldn't say that to her face. She is very sensitive and would start to cry. She should go on a diet. I can't understand how such a fat person can swim. Why doesn't she sink to the bottom of the pool? Some day I will ask Marty about that.

140

Sondra and Jane threw their clothes in a pile on the floor but Mouse folded everything and packed it away in her overnight case. Then she took out a small notebook and said, 'Let's make a Slam Book.'

'What's that?' Jane said.

I was glad she asked because I didn't know either. I figured I would tell Mouse that the reason I didn't know about Slam Books is that I haven't made one in years because where I live that is just for babies.

Mouse told us, 'Slam Books are great fun. You'll see.' She was busy writing something down in her notebook. We sat in a circle around her and waited.

In a minute she held up a piece of paper and said, 'This is a sample list. All of us fill it in about each other. It's the only way to find out what your friends really think of you!'

I looked at the sample list. It said: Name,

Hair, Face, Body, Brain, Best thing, Worst thing and In general.

'You see,' Mouse explained, 'we'd never be brave enough to just sit around and tell each other the truth about ourselves. That would be too embarrassing. But since everybody wants to know what other people really think of them, this is an easy way to find out. You can start with me if you want. I'll go stand in the hall and you fill in the list. Later, when we've all had our chance, we get to read about ourselves in private.' Mouse walked to my bedroom door. 'Remember,' she told us, 'you've got to be honest or it won't do any of us any good.' She opened the door and stepped out into the hall.

'Well,' I said, 'who wants to go first?'

'You start, Sheila,' Jane said. 'It's your party.'

'OK, give me the book.'

Before I had a chance to begin, my bedroom

door opened and Mouse poked her head in. 'I forgot to tell you . . . when you're done filling it in, you fold the page over so nobody can see what you wrote.'

'OK . . . OK . . .' I said.

'I just thought you should know,' Mouse told me, closing the door again.

I filled in the list one-two-three. I wrote:

name	Mouse Ellis
hair	needs washing
face	only a mother could love it
body	too many scabs
brain	pretty good
best thing	can do everything!
worst thing	knows it! ! ! ! !
in general	my best friend and lots of fun

I folded my part of the page over so the others couldn't see it and passed it to Sondra. When she was done she passed it to Jane, and then we called Mouse back into the room and Sondra went out.

While Sondra was in the hall Mom came upstairs to tell us she and Daddy were going into town to pick up some pizza for our snack. 'We'll be back in less than an hour,' Mom said. 'Libby and Maryann are home in case you need anything.'

'OK . . . we'll be fine,' I said, anxious to get back to the Slam Book.

When we were done writing about Sondra it was my turn to leave the room. I knew I didn't have to worry about what my friends think of me, because I am careful to keep my bad points to myself. Sometimes I think I am really two people. I am the only one who knows Sheila Tubman. Everyone else knows only SHEILA THE GREAT.

Jane was the last one to stand out in the hall, and when we were through writing about her she came back into my room. Then Mouse tore out a page for each of us to read privately. She said we should sit by ourselves and face the wall in case we didn't want anyone to see our expression.

We all laughed at that but did it anyway. I sat on my bed with my back to the others. I unfolded my paper so I could see all three opinions of me at once.

Who did they think they were? Why did I ever bother to invite them to my house? They didn't deserve it! I read about myself six times, but I didn't turn away from the wall.

After a little while I noticed that the room was very quiet. I wondered what the others were thinking. That's when Sondra started to cry. I knew it was her even though I was facing the wall. First she cried low, but when I turned around to look at her she took her hands away

name	Sheila Tubman	Sheila Tubman	Sheila Tubman
hair	parted crooked	should grow longer	much too long
face	ugly but lovable	weird eyebrows	gruesome!
body	skin & bones	ugly feet	abnormal!!!
brain	thinks it knows it all	a mental	OVERUSED!!!!!!!
best thing	picks neat friends	gives parties	???????????
worst thing	CHICKEN	bossy	acts real tuff!
in general	an interesting person	not that bad	there's hope

from her mouth and started bawling so loud you could probably hear it a mile away.

'I hate you!' she yelled. 'Every single one of you. You all think I'm a big, fat slob! Even my own sister thinks I'm a fat slob!'

'Well, you are!' Jane said. 'And you should do something about it. Anyway, somebody said some pretty bad things about me too. Like I can't keep secrets and my brain is turned off most of the time!'

'So?' Mouse said. 'I don't think it was fair of you to make fun of my scabs!'

'I didn't make fun of your scabs!' Jane hollered.

'Somebody did!'

'Well, it wasn't me!' Jane yelled.

I didn't say anything because I was the one who wrote that about Mouse's scabs. But I never thought it would bother her so much.

'And another thing,' Mouse said. 'I don't

think any of you have the right to tell me that my hair needs washing!'

'What's so bad about that?' Sondra asked. 'How do you think I feel that two of you wrote I'm a crybaby!'

'You are a crybaby!' Mouse told her. 'And I don't see what business it is of yours that my belly button sticks out.'

'I didn't write that!' Sondra said. 'I wrote about your ears.'

'Well, that's just as dumb!'

'I'm the one who wrote about your belly button,' Jane said. 'And it does stick out! So there!'

'Just shut up, Jane!' Mouse hollered.

Jane was standing near my dresser and when Mouse said that Jane picked up one of Bobby Egran's model aeroplanes and threw it across the room at her. 'Who's going to make me?' she asked.

'You cut that out!' I told her. 'They're not mine.'

'So?' Jane said, throwing a plane at me.

'I told you to cut that out!' I shouted. 'And I want to know which one of you wrote that my body is abnormal! My body is as normal as any of yours. Even more normal because I don't have to hide in any closet when I get undressed. And who says I have ugly feet? Your feet are just as ugly!'

'I wrote about your feet,' Sondra said. 'Because your big toes are funny-looking. I think there's something wrong with them!'

'How dare you say that about my feet!' I yelled. 'You big, fat crybaby!'

'I'm going home,' Sondra bawled. 'I don't have to stay here and listen to this.'

'That's right,' Jane told her. 'Go running home to Mama. Just like always.' She tossed a model boat at Sondra.

'I could tell plenty about you if I felt like it,' Sondra said, throwing the model back at Jane.

'You just try it and I'll get you!' Jane yelled, as she flung another model.

This time Sondra picked it up and sent it flying across the room at Jane. And Mouse picked one up and did the same thing. I got so mad I yelled, 'You're ruining my party!' And I threw one of Bobby's models at Jane.

Pretty soon we were all throwing the models at each other and we were all screaming and half-crying too, because of the terrible things we wrote about each other, even though some of them were true.

That's when Libby opened the door and said, 'What is going on in here?'

I shouted, 'Get out and mind your own business!'

Jane threw a model at Libby and Libby had to

150

duck so it wouldn't hit her in the head. Instead it hit Maryann, who was standing right behind Libby. She hollered, 'You little brats! You little baby brats! You're too young for a slumber party!'

'I said get out of my room now!'

'I am going to tell Mother and Father about this, Sheila.'

'Blah blah blah,' I said.

'Yeah,' Mouse told them, 'blah blah blah!'

Then Mouse looked at me and we started to laugh. And when we did Jane did too. And after a minute even Sondra joined us. We all laughed at Libby and Maryann as we shouted, 'Blah blah blah blah blah!'

Libby called us 'baby brats' one more time before she slammed our door shut. Then I flopped down on my bed and looked around at my room. Bobby's models were all over the place. 'He's going to get me.'

'Don't be silly,' Mouse said.

'He said he would and he means it. I know he means it!'

'So what? Who cares about the old model maniac?' Mouse asked.

'That's easy for you to say,' I told her. 'You're not the one he's going to get. There's only one thing to do.'

'What's that?' Sondra asked.

'We have to fix up every single model.'

'But how can we?' Sondra said. 'One of them broke right in half.'

'That one we can throw in the garbage. But the rest of them we have to repair.' I went to the desk and opened the drawer. I took out two tubes of Testor's glue and a box of model paints. I divided the models into three piles. 'It won't take long to fix them up,' I said.

An hour later we were still sitting on the floor gluing and painting when my mother knocked

152

on my door and called, 'Snack time.'

I whispered, 'Quick . . . hide the stuff,' as I ran across my room to open the door for Mom. She was carrying a big tray of pizza.

'Ummm . . . that smells delicious,' Sondra said.

'It's nice and hot,' Mom told us. She set it down on the desk. Then she wriggled her nose and looked around. 'Something smells funny in here, girls.'

'It does?' I asked.

'Yes, like glue or something.'

'Oh, that's just my toothpaste, Mrs Tubman,' Mouse said.

'What kind of toothpaste smells like that?' Mom asked.

'This new kind that prevents cavities,' Mouse told her.

'I hope it tastes better than it smells,' Mom said.

'Mother . . . Mother . . . is that you?' Libby called.

'Yes,' Mom said, 'we have plenty of pizza.'

Libby came rushing into my room with Maryann right behind her. 'Mother, Sheila and her friends were just awful while you were gone. They were yelling and screaming and throwing around all the models from the top of the dresser.'

Mom stood in my doorway and said, 'Sheila, what's this all about?'

'I told you she'd ruin my party,' I said. 'She just has to butt in on everything!'

Mom looked over at my dresser. 'Where are all of Bobby's models?'

'Under the bed, Mrs Tubman,' Mouse said. 'We wanted to make sure nothing would happen to them, so we put them away for the night.'

'They are impossible children, Mother,' Libby said.

Mom looked back at us. We all smiled at her. 'This is Sheila's party, Libby. I think you and Maryann should go to your room and let these girls take care of themselves. I know they wouldn't do anything destructive to another person's property.'

'Oh, Mother!' Libby said. 'You don't understand at all!'

'Goodnight, Libby. Goodnight, Maryann,' Mom told them.

'Thanks, Mom,' I said.

'Have a good time, but don't stay up too late.'

When Mom went downstairs we started on the pizza. Sondra ate two pieces and reached for a third, but we all shook our heads at her and she took her hand away and said, 'The truth really hurts!' We all agreed.

After our snack we went back to work on Bobby's models. We fixed them up pretty good.

From far away you'd never know there was anything wrong with them. And besides, didn't he say he was bringing home a whole bunch of new ones? So he'll probably never notice that these have been in battle. At least I hope he won't!

We spread the models out to dry and put away the glue and paints. 'I'm getting tired,' Sondra said.

'We can't go to bed yet,' Mouse told her. 'We still have some unfinished business to take care of.'

'What?' Sondra said.

I looked at Mouse because I knew what she was thinking. 'We have to get even with Libby and Maryann for telling on us.'

'Goody!' Jane said. 'They deserve the worst!'

'But what's the worst?' Sondra asked.

'We should put frogs in their beds,' Mouse said.

156

'Where are we supposed to get frogs?' Jane asked.

'Behind my house,' Mouse said. 'There's a brook full of them.'

'Forget it,' I said. 'My mother's not going to let us go running around at this hour.'

'Then we'll have to think up something else,' Mouse said. 'But it's got to be really great!'

'I know,' I said. 'We'll decorate the toilet seat with toothpaste and the first one of them to sit down will get full of it . . . you know where!'

'Hey, that's a neat idea, Sheila,' Mouse said. 'How'd you think that up?'

'When your brain *knows it all* it's easy!' I told her. I could tell from Mouse's expression that she was the one who wrote that about me. But I didn't care, because she also wrote that I am an interesting person and I like that idea a lot. Even Sondra and Jane wrote that in general I am OK. And that's what counts. So what if they

think I'm bossy sometimes? It's only because I know more than they do. So what if I have weird eyebrows and funny toes? Not that I agree, because I don't see anything weird about my eyebrows and my toes are just like everybody else's toes. But to be an interesting person! Well, not everyone can be that. That is something special!

We all went into the hall bathroom and brushed our teeth and used the toilet. Then I personally covered the toilet seat with toothpaste. When I was finished the others wanted to add a little to it, so by the time we were done there wasn't a spot on it without toothpaste.

We went back to my room and waited. When my bedroom door is open you can hear the water running in the bathroom.

Pretty soon we heard Libby and Maryann walking down the hall.

'They're going to the bathroom now,' Jane said.

'*Shush*,' I told her. I think they brushed their teeth first and then it sounded like one of them was gargling. It was hard to keep from laughing because we knew in another minute Libby or Maryann would be sitting down on all that toothpaste.

But then we heard the toilet flush without a sound from either one.

'I don't get it,' Mouse whispered.

'They probably didn't go yet,' I whispered back. 'Maybe they just flushed a tissue or something.'

We waited some more and the toilet flushed again. But still no sound from either one of them.

'Maybe they go standing up,' Mouse said.

'Why should they?' I asked. 'Our toilets are clean.'

'Maybe they used your mother's bathroom instead,' Sondra said.

'No . . . Libby never uses my mother's bathroom.'

'Well, I don't know,' Mouse said, peeking out into the hall, 'but they're on their way back to Libby's room.'

'It doesn't make sense,' I said.

'It doesn't make sense at all,' Mouse, Sondra and Jane agreed.

I got into bed and the others snuggled into their sleeping bags. 'We'll get them tomorrow,' I said. 'They'll be sorry they told on us!'

We giggled for a long time before we fell asleep.

The next morning I got up early and looked down at my friends. They were sound asleep. I had to go to the bathroom so I got out of bed and tiptoed down the hall. I forgot about the

160

toothpaste until I sat down on the toilet. It was still sticky. It got all over my backside. I couldn't even get it off with paper. And it itched too. So I decided to take a shower. But when I turned on the water it came out icy cold and I screamed so loud I woke everyone up.

Daddy and Mom, Libby and Maryann, Sondra, Jane and Mouse all came running down the hall.

I covered myself up with a big towel and told them, 'The water was very cold.'

Mom said, 'Sheila, why on earth were you going to take a shower this early in the morning?'

'To get the toothpaste off me,' I told her.

As soon as I said that Libby and Maryann started laughing. I stuck my tongue out at them.

'What toothpaste?' Mom asked.

Mouse said, 'You see, Mrs Tubman, Sheila had a lot of mosquito bites and my mother

always says toothpaste will stop them from itching.'

'So I spread toothpaste all over me,' I said. 'But now I want to wash it off.'

'Is that your new toothpaste, Mouse?' Mom asked. 'The one that smells like glue?'

'It doesn't matter what kind of toothpaste you use, Mrs Tubman,' Mouse said. 'Any old kind will do.'

'I never heard of putting toothpaste on mosquito bites,' Mom said. 'Next time I get one I'll have to try it.'

That night, after my friends went home, Daddy asked, 'Did you have a nice party, Sheila?'

'Oh yes!' I told him. 'My slumber party was the best slumber party that ever was. Just like I knew it would be!'

'That's good,' Daddy said, slapping the back of his neck. 'Whew . . . I've got some really bad

mosquito bites. Sheila, would you run upstairs and get me the toothpaste?'

'Don't bother, Daddy,' I said, starting to laugh. 'It really doesn't help at all!'

14
Under the Hay

Libby is in love, for a change. This time he is fourteen and he works the movie projector at camp. His name is Hank Crane. I wonder if he is related to Ichabod. I asked Libby about that, but all she said was, 'Sheila, you are very weird!'

On rainy days we see old movies at camp. Last week it rained and me and Mouse watched Libby instead of the movie. She sat right up close to Hank and we're not sure but we think they kissed a couple of times. I would love to tell my mother. But I'm afraid Libby would get me. She might let Jennifer loose or something.

When it isn't raining Hank is busy with his movie camera. He is making an original film

of us at our activities. One day he spent a lot of time at pottery. He asked me to do some silly things, like putting clay on my head while I pretended to be the pottery wheel. Naturally I refused. So he got Russ to do it. I can't imagine what Hank's film is going to be like. I have the feeling I will never find out because I don't think it will ever be finished.

Libby says that Hank is very talented, which is more important than being good-looking. Even Maryann Markman likes him. I think he is really dumb to pick Libby instead of Maryann.

Next week is our last week of day camp. When it is over Marty says I have to take my swimming test. I know I will drown if he makes me swim across the pool. Then everyone will be sorry they forced me to learn to swim!

Mouse and the twins don't bother swimming

regular any more. They are too busy doing handstands and somersaults under the water. I will never be able to do tricks. I think I would be better off just staying far, far away from oceans, lakes and pools for the rest of my life.

On Friday night we are going on a hayride. Everyone from camp is invited. We are dividing up into two groups since we can't all fit into one wagon. Libby is very happy about this because she doesn't want to be in the same wagon as me. And I know why! She wants to be alone with Hank Crane! Well, I don't care. Who wants to waste a good hayride looking at Libby? I have never been on a hayride, anyway. Mouse hasn't either. But she says we will have lots of fun.

Libby spent all Friday afternoon getting beautiful. She even put on clean jeans and cut her toenails. Mr Ellis called for us at 8.30 and dropped us off at camp.

The wagons were already there and kids

were piling in. We were supposed to divide up by age. So Libby didn't have to worry after all. Denise was in charge of our wagon. One thing that surprised me was the horses. I didn't know they were going to pull our wagon. I thought it would be attached to a car. I am not too crazy about horses. Suppose they jump up in the air and we all fall out of the wagon? Or worse yet – they could go wild and pull us into the woods!

As I was thinking about whether or not I should really go Mouse said, 'Come on, Sheila . . . let's get a good place up front.'

'Up front' means near the horses, I found out. 'I don't think this is the best place to sit,' I said. 'Let's get more in the middle.'

'No . . . No . . .'Mouse said. 'You have the best fun up here.'

'How do you know? You've never been on a hayride. You said so yourself!'

'My mother told me,' Mouse said.

'Oh. How many hayrides has she been on?'

'In the olden days, when she was a girl, she went on lots of them.'

'Oh.'

The first thing I found out was hay isn't soft like I thought it would be. It is kind of sharp and it makes some people sneeze. Sam Sweeney started sneezing as soon as he sat down.

Our hayride began at nine. By then it was dark. Libby's wagon went first and ours followed. Denise brought along her guitar and we started singing right away. She played her Anne Boleyn song first to get us into the mood. After a while she said she would tell us a ghost story. I don't like ghost stories, so I decided not to listen. I can do that if I really concentrate, but it isn't easy. I have to think of other things the whole time the person is talking. I do it in school sometimes if the lesson gets boring. But

it's harder to do on a hayride than in school.

We turned off the main road on to an old bumpy one. There were no street lights and it was very dark. There wasn't any moon in the sky and I was glad. Especially that there wasn't a full moon. Because werewolves only come out when the moon is full. Not that there's really any such thing as werewolves – I know there isn't – but still it was better that there was no moon.

Mouse leaned close and whispered, 'This is Old Sleepy Hollow Road . . . the one where Ichabod Crane saw the Headless Horseman.'

'It is?' I asked.

'Yes. And see up there . . . that's the little church with the graveyard behind it. That's where the Horseman comes from.'

Denise finished her story. It was very quiet, except for Sam's sneezes. There were a lot of giggles. I think everybody was a little bit scared.

I pretended we weren't on Old Sleepy Hollow Road. I wished I was home in my bed with the covers over my ear. I don't know why I ever came on this hayride in the first place. As we got closer to the church I heard the noise. It couldn't possibly be him, could it? There isn't any such thing as the Headless Horseman. I know that!

The next time I heard the noise there was a flash in the sky. Oh no! It was thundering. We were going to have a storm! And here I am, out in the open, I thought. Out in a dumb old hay wagon! The lightning will probably scare the horses and they'll run wild – right into the woods – where the Headless Horseman will be waiting!

My heart started beating like mad and I was full of sweat. I couldn't stand it any more. The only thing to do was bury myself under the hay. Then I'd be safe. Safe from the lightning and

the horses running wild and the terrible dark woods and the Horseman.

'Sheila, what are you doing?' Mouse asked. 'Sheila . . . come out of there. Are you crazy or something?' She tried to dig me out of the hay, but I wouldn't let her. Why should I come out? Let Mouse and the others get struck by lightning. Let them fall out of the wagon when the horses run wild. Let them get lost in the woods with the Headless Horseman!

'Denise . . .' I heard Mouse call. 'Denise, help me. Sheila's under the hay and she won't come out.'

I kicked my legs at her. They weren't going to get me out. Oh no! I was staying buried until I was home where it was safe.

But Denise is much bigger than me, and stronger too. 'Sheila Tubman,' she said, pulling me out, 'what do you think you're doing?'

'It's going to rain,' I told her. 'I'm just getting

ready for it. I don't want to get wet like the rest of you. So just leave me alone. I like it under the hay.'

'You're really funny,' Mouse said.

'No I'm not,' I told her. 'I'm interesting, that's all.'

'You can say that again,' Mouse laughed.

'Anyway,' Denise said, 'I don't think it's going to rain. The storm seems to have passed.' She pointed to the sky. 'You see . . . the moon's out over there.'

I looked up and saw that she was right. There was a big, full moon! I kept my eyes shut for the rest of the ride. I wasn't taking any chances. If a werewolf ran out of the woods I wasn't going to be the one to see him!

Finally, we made it back to camp. I was never so happy to see Daddy in my life. 'How was it?' he asked. 'Did you have lots of fun?'

Mouse answered. She said, 'It was great fun,

172

Mr Tubman. Just great! Wasn't it, Sheila?'

I tried a smile. 'Oh sure,' I said. 'Great.'

Now that I have been on one hayride, I don't think I will be in a hurry to go on another.

15
Sheila the Great!

This afternoon I am going to take my swimming test. I hope it rains. I hope it rains and pours until we leave here. But when I checked the sky the sun was shining. And when I turned on the radio and listened to the weather report there was no rain forecast.

So I hope I get sick and the doctor says I can't go in the water for ten days. But I feel fine. Except for my stomach, which keeps jumping all around.

So I hope that when I get to the pool this afternoon Marty won't be there. And no one will be able to find him. Then I will never have to take my swimming test!

But when we got to the pool Marty was there,

174

waiting for me. That's when I knew there was no getting out of it. I would have to take my Beginner's Test and if I drowned, I drowned! It was better not to think about it. Besides, chances were I wouldn't drown. Marty would probably save me. But if he had to jump in and save me in front of everyone, that would be as bad as drowning. Maybe even worse!

When I was in my suit Mom said, 'Good luck, Sheila. And please don't be nervous.'

'Me . . . nervous?' I said. 'Ha ha. That's really funny.'

When Marty saw me he called, 'Hi, Sheila. All set?'

I didn't answer him.

'OK, now here's all you have to do,' Marty said. 'First you'll jump in and swim across the deep end of the pool. Then you'll tread water for two minutes.'

I don't know who Marty thought he was

fooling. If he expected me to jump in and swim across the deep end of the pool he was even nuttier than I thought. He was more than nutty. He was even more than crazy! He was also stupid, dumb, and an idiot!

'Are you listening to me?' Marty asked.

'Oh sure,' I told him, 'I'm listening. But you know I can't swim across the whole pool!'

'Yes you can,' Marty said.

I folded my arms and gave him one of my best stares.

'You've got to try, Sheila. That's all I ask. You just can't give up without trying.'

'Who's giving up?' I asked. 'I can swim. You know that. You've seen me.'

'OK,' Marty said. 'So I know it. So now I want you to prove it to everyone by swimming across the pool.'

'Maybe I just don't feel like it.'

'Look, Sheila, there's absolutely nothing to

be afraid of. If you can't make it I'll be right there to help you.'

'I am not afraid!'

'Then prove that you're not! Jump in right now and start swimming. I know you can make it. I have a lot of confidence in you.'

I didn't answer him.

'Please, Sheila. Please try . . . for me.'

I liked the way Marty said that. But when I looked across the pool the other side seemed ten miles away. 'You promise nothing bad will happen?' I asked.

'I promise,' Marty said. 'Word of honour. I'll even clear this section of the pool while you take your test.'

'Do I have to keep my face in the water the whole time?'

'No, you can swim any way you want.'

'How far is it across? About a mile?'

Marty laughed. 'It's only forty feet.'

'It looks like ten miles to me,' I said.

'It's not. Tell you what . . . I'll count to three. Then you jump in and start swimming. I'll walk along the side of the pool and if you have any trouble I'll pull you out.'

'You'll really be near me?'

'Yes. I told you that. Now get ready.'

I stood at the edge of the pool.

Marty counted. 'One . . . and two . . . and three . . . jump!'

I didn't move.

'What are you waiting for?' Marty asked.

'I wasn't quite ready,' I told him. 'Let's try it again.'

'OK. Here we go. And one . . . and two . . . and three . . . jump!'

I held my nose and jumped in. When I came up I looked for Marty. He was right where he said he'd be. 'Swim . . . swim . . .' he called.

I started. First I tried blowing bubbles, but I

felt like I wasn't getting anywhere. So I kept my head out and swam like a dog. That way I could see what was going on. And I could keep an eye on Marty to make sure he followed me all the way across.

Every time I looked up at him he yelled, 'Go, Sheila, go!'

I swam past the low diving board. Then past the high one. And then I started to get tired. I couldn't get my arms all the way out of the water. And my legs didn't want to kick any more. I looked up at Marty.

'Go, Sheila, go! Don't stop now!'

Marty was wrong. The pool wasn't forty feet across. It was really forty miles. I never should have tried it.

'Go . . . go . . .'

Why didn't he just shut up? When I raised my head and looked straight across the pool, who did I see waiting for me but Mouse and

the twins. They were yelling 'Go . . . go!' just like Marty. I wanted to tell them to stop. That I would never get to their side. This was very stupid. Soon I would be dead. Why didn't Marty pull me out? What was he waiting for? Couldn't he see I wasn't going to make it?

I tried to say, 'I can't make it,' but it came out so soft he didn't hear me.

He said, 'That's it. Keep on going . . .'

I can't . . . I can't . . . I thought. Then my hand touched the ladder.

Mouse and the twins were cheering and jumping up and down. Marty was yelling, 'You made it! You made it! I knew you would!'

It was true. I swam across the deep end of the pool and I was still alive! I really and truly did it! I tried to climb up the ladder, but Marty bent down and said, 'Now all you've got to do is tread water for two minutes.'

'No . . . no . . . let me up!'

'Relax, Sheila. You can do it. Just tread for two minutes.'

Treading water is pretty easy. It's just like riding a bicycle except you aren't on one. But I was so tired. I wanted to go to sleep.

Marty was holding a watch. He talked to me the whole time I was treading. He said, 'That's it, Sheila. Only one more minute to go. And what's one little minute?'

When we got down to the last couple of seconds Marty counted out loud. 'Ten, nine, eight, seven, six, five, four, three, two, one . . . Hurray! You did it! You did it!'

I climbed up the ladder and Marty put his arms around me. Then he gave me a big kiss right in front of everybody, but I didn't mind. My mother ran over and wrapped me up in a towel and Mouse and the twins dragged a lounge chair to me.

'I really did it?' I asked over and over.

'You sure did,' Marty said.

'How about that?' Never mind that Mouse and the twins are already working on their Advanced cards. Never mind that Libby is practically a Junior Life Saver. Never mind that I will never dive like Betsy Ellis or stand on my hands under the water. *I can swim.* I proved it to everyone, including myself! I am Sunny Tubman, girl swimmer! I am Super Sheila the Swimming Wonder. I am . . . I am . . . I am . . .

'Sheila . . .' I heard my mother say. 'Are you all right?'

I think I nodded.

Then another voice laughed and said, 'She's asleep. That's all.'

I think it was Marty. But I couldn't even open my eyes to thank him.

16
Farewell to Tarrytown

Next week we are going home. Our summer in Tarrytown is practically over. In some ways I am glad. Such as I won't have to listen for the Headless Horseman any more. But in other ways I'm sorry. I will really miss Mouse. She's promised to tell Bobby Egran that I never touched any of his models. But just in case he doesn't believe her and decides to *get me*, Mouse will say I've gone to Australia and won't be back.

'I'll visit you in the city,' Mouse said. 'And next summer maybe you'll come back to Tarrytown.'

'But next summer we're going to Disneyland,' I told her.

'You're really going?' she asked.

'Well, we're thinking about it. At least I am!'

'Then I'll think about it too,' Mouse said. 'And maybe we can all go together.'

'Now that's a really good idea!' I said.

Me and Mouse would love to be around when Libby says goodbye to Hank Crane. She is the star of his new movie. It's all about a girl who sees everything upside down. Libby had to learn to stand on her head to get the feel of the part. She says some day Hank will be very famous and we will all be able to say we-knew-him-when . . . Mouse and I don't believe her.

Mom got the idea of having a Farewell to Tarrytown party. She told us about it after supper tonight.

Daddy said, 'That sounds like fun.'

'Can I invite Mouse?' I asked.

'Of course,' Mom said. 'We'll have the whole Ellis family.'

Then Libby asked, 'Can I invite Hank and Maryann Markman?'

Mom said, 'Sure. And let's have Marty too.'

'And the Van Arden twins,' I said.

'And maybe Hank can bring a friend for Maryann,' Libby said.

By that time Daddy and Mom were laughing and making up a party list.

The next few days we were all busy planning our Farewell to Tarrytown. Daddy said he would do the cooking on the outside grill and Mom said we'd set up tables and chairs in the backyard.

At the last minute I remembered about Betsy Ellis and how she gets hives from dogs, but Daddy said she would be all right as long as she didn't get near Jennifer.

The day of our party started out cloudy and

Mom was very disappointed. I thought if it rained we could get up a good game of indoor hide-and-seek. But by noon the sun came out and Mom cheered up.

At two o'clock our first guests came – Mouse and her family. Betsy was dragging Ootch. But she had a new ribbon tied around him instead of the dirty old string.

Right after that everyone started to arrive at once. The Van Arden twins, Maryann Markman, Hank and his friend Bucky Parker, who brought a bat, a ball and a fielder's mitt with him.

Marty came last and for a minute I didn't recognize him. It was the first time I saw him in clothes instead of a bathing suit!

We spent the afternoon eating – hamburgers, hot dogs, barbecued chicken and a bunch of stuff to go with it. Everyone took turns at the grill so Daddy didn't have to cook the whole time. We all agreed that Hank Crane and Bucky

Parker were the best cooks. They were the only ones who didn't drop anything into the fire or burn up the rolls.

Even Jennifer had fun. All of our guests stopped to say hello and tell her congratulations on her condition. Towards the middle of the afternoon she curled up in the shade and went to sleep.

At six o'clock Mom brought out the watermelons. Me, Mouse and the twins took our plates and went off by ourselves. When we finished eating Mouse said, 'Now take three pips and stick them to your foreheads. Then give each pip a boy's name, and the one that stays on the longest is the boy you'll marry.'

I couldn't think of one boy I might want to marry. So I named my pips Russ Bindel, Sam Sweeney and Bobby Egran.

After Mouse, Sondra and Jane named their pips we all stood up and walked around with

them stuck to our foreheads. As they dried they fell off. Sam Sweeney fell off me first, then Russ Bindel, which left me with Bobby Egran as the boy I would marry. And that was pretty funny because I don't even want to meet him, let alone marry him!

Then Bucky Parker started throwing his baseball around and pretty soon we divided into teams and started a game. Me, Mouse, Bucky and Marty against Sondra, Jane, Libby, Maryann and Hank.

As soon as we got started Betsy burst into tears. 'I want to play too!' she cried.

Since our team only had four and the other team had five we got Betsy. When it was her turn to bat all she did was stand there and laugh. Finally Marty called her out on strikes.

I struck out swinging my first two times up but the third time around I hit a fly ball towards first base, which Libby dropped. Before

she could pick it up I was safe at first. And that's when I noticed Jennifer's friend. He was running around in the bushes. He was practically next to me. I remembered the last time he saw me and what happened. So I stood very still and prayed that he would go away.

'Why are you staring like that?' Libby asked me.

'Jennifer's friend is back,' I said. 'Look . . .'

Libby turned around and saw him. She called, 'Time out . . .' and dived into the bushes after the dog.

Then a man came into our yard calling, 'Mumford . . . Mumford . . . here, boy.'

When Jennifer's friend heard that he ran out of the bushes and barked like crazy. Jennifer must have recognized his bark, because she woke up and got so excited she wrapped herself around the tree. So Daddy had to unchain her and when he did she took off and ran for her friend.

189

Mrs Ellis hollered, 'Betsy, get into the house . . . hurry, or you'll get your hives!'

The man kept saying, 'I'm terribly sorry. Really, I am. I had no idea you were having a party. And I don't know why he ran off like that.'

My father introduced himself to the man and said it was all right about his dog. Then the man told Daddy his name was Cyrus Beldrich and his dog was Mumford.

Mom gave Mr Beldrich a big piece of watermelon and told him that Jennifer is going to be a mother and that Mumford is the father. Mr Beldrich sat down saying, 'Imagine that!' While he ate his watermelon Jennifer and Mumford sniffed each other.

Mouse said, 'Well, now the Egrans won't have any trouble naming the puppies. They can make up combinations of Jennifer and Mumford.'

'Like Jennimum,' Jane said.

'Or Mumifer,' Sondra said.

'How about Mumfy?' Mouse asked.

'Or Jake!' Sondra laughed.

'That's not a combination of Jennifer and Mumford,' Mouse said.

'But it sounds nice,' Sondra told her.

'Which one do you like best, Sheila?' Mouse asked.

'Oh . . . I think I'll take Jake!' I said.

Then we all laughed some more until I remembered that I was in the backyard with two dogs loose! So I ran for the house, calling, 'I'll get hives! I'll get awful, huge, giant hives!'

But when I got inside I thought about having a puppy named Jake who would be a much nicer, better dog than Peter Hatcher's.

Except of course that dogs don't like me.

So how can we possibly have one?

Even if he is small and soft and his name is Jake.

It is out of the question.

But suppose Libby gets her own way?

Oh well, I will worry about that when the time comes!

About the Author

Judy Blume spent her childhood in Elizabeth, New Jersey, making up stories inside her head. She has spent her adult years in many places, doing the same thing, only now she writes her stories down on paper. More than 82 million copies of her books have been sold, in thirty-two languages. Her twenty-eight books have won many awards, including the National Book Foundation's Medal for Distinguished Contribution to American Literature.

Judy lives in Key West, Florida, and New York City with her husband. She loves her readers and is happy to hear from them. You can visit her at JudyBlume.com, follow @JudyBlume on Twitter or join her at Judy Blume on Facebook.

Judy Blume

TALES of A FOURTH GRADE NOTHING

FUDGE IS PETER'S NAUGHTY LITTLE BROTHER AND ONE BIG HEAP OF TROUBLE!

Disaster follows Fudge wherever he goes.
And Peter's usually the only one who can sort out
the mess. Fudge gets all the attention, all the time.
It's enough to drive an older brother mad!

Judy Blume

A FUDGE BOOK

SUPERFUDGE

When Fudge discovers that his new baby sister
is too small to play with him, he tries to sell her.
When that doesn't work, he tries to give her away.
And then on his first day at school Fudge has a
run-in with his teacher and calls her Rat Face.
Can his big brother help him out yet again?

www.GOBSTOPPERBOOKS.com

VISIT THE **GOBSTOPPERS** WEBSITE FOR

A...HOR NEWS · ...ONT...NTENT

...IDEOS · GAMES · PR...S...

AND MORE

MACMILLAN
Children's Books